She had so many questions, and not all of them pertained to ██ ██ ar.

She wanted to understa █████████████████ go out of his wa █████████████████ of man who, wa █████████████████ brother. The kind █████████████████ ing back through her ████████████ her.

But Anna's question ████████ to remain unanswered. Right ███, she needed to focus on five-year-old Ali.

Anna did plan to thank David again for his help in getting Ali here. And she hoped David would open up to her about more than just the little boy. Anna had a feeling David could use a friend. Maybe she was just imagining the way his dark eyes gleamed with interest when he looked at her. But every time he glanced her way, he was smiling.

* * *

Books by Lenora Worth

LENORA WORTH

has written more than thirty books, most of those for Steeple Hill. She also works freelance for a local magazine, where she had written monthly opinion columns, feature articles and social commentaries. She also wrote for the local paper for five years. Married to her high school sweetheart for thirty-two years, Lenora lives in Louisiana and has two grown children and a cat. She loves to read, take long walks and sit in her garden.

Lone Star Secret
Lenora Worth

Steeple
Hill®

Published by Steeple Hill Books™

Special thanks and acknowledgment to Lenora Worth for her contribution to the Homecoming Heroes miniseries.

STEEPLE HILL BOOKS

Steeple
Hill®

ISBN-13: 978-0-373-87492-7
ISBN-10:   0-373-87492-8

LONE STAR SECRET

Printed in U.S.A.

Why did you flee away secretly, and steal away from me, and not tell me; for I might have sent you away with joy and songs, with timbrel and harp?
—*Genesis* 31:27–28

To all the soldiers—those who have sacrificed for my freedom and those who are still fighting today. God bless you all.

Chapter One

Chief Warrant Officer David Ryland glanced around the sterile waiting room at Fort Bonnell Medical Center, taking in the crowd of well-wishers gathered around the little boy on the stretcher. The circuslike atmosphere made him feel a bit frazzled and edgy, but then he'd just landed on American soil—on good ol' Texas soil—after flying medevac Black Hawks for eighteen months in the war-torn Middle East. He had a right to be edgy.

Moving his gaze from the excited group hovering near the doctor and little Ali Tabiz Willis, David found himself staring straight into the blue-green eyes of Anna Terenkov. Anna looked away, then quickly glanced back at David, a slight smile on her heart-shaped face.

David studied her closely, deciding he'd better dust off his social skills now that he was home. And his flirting skills. Because he definitely wanted to get to know the woman responsible for helping to make this day happen. David had heard about the legendary humanitarian who ran the Children of the Day charity, but seeing her in person was a whole different matter. She was not what he had expected.

She was even better.

Her blond hair was pulled back in a haphazard coil held up by an intricate silver clip. She was petite, but her calm, assured presence made her seem taller. She wore loose-fitting green cargo pants and a crisp white button-up blouse. And around her neck she wore a choker-style strand of dark leather, from which hung a chunky sterling-silver pendant with the cross and the lance of Golgotha set against an etched background. He couldn't move his gaze from her.

Caitlyn Villard, the Care Coordinator for Children of the Day, and Army Chaplain Steve Windham introduced Caitlyn's twin nieces to Ali. While the precocious five-year-olds wished him well in Arabic and English, David watched Anna's face. She lit up around children, her smile turning to sunshine. He'd noticed that the minute he'd exited the plane with little Ali earlier that morning.

"CW3 David Ryland, ma'am," David had said by way of a greeting back at the airfield. "Delivering one Ali Tabiz, as ordered."

Anna grinned as she studied the three square bars on his insignia. "It wasn't exactly an order, Chief. More of a hope sent out on a wing and a prayer."

David nodded, liking the way the slight lilt of her

foreign accent mixed nicely with a little bit of Texas twang. He'd learned in all the back and forth coordination for Ali's trip that she was Russian and had lived there until her early teens, when her father had been killed in Afghanistan.

"Well, I got the wings secured and I guess you took care of the prayer, ma'am."

She touched her fingers to the cross at her neck. "We all had a big part in that." Reaching out to shake his hand, she said, "Thank you so much. And please don't call me ma'am. I'm Anna."

"You're welcome, Anna," David replied, the warmth of her energy shooting through his tired, travel-worn system.

She held his hand, cupping it between both of hers. "I'm not just thanking you for helping Ali, sir. Thanks for serving our country, too."

David was both humbled and shaken by her sincere, misty-eyed gratitude. "Okay, if I can't call you ma'am, then you sure don't have to address me as sir."

She nodded. "Then I'll just call you Chief."

David laughed. "From what I hear, you're the real chief around here."

She shook her head. "No, just someone who understands that war is devastating to children."

All of the activity around them had blurred into the background. He could hear the sounds of other soldiers coming off the jet, the cries of family members who'd been waiting for their loved ones to come home. He could feel the way the hot August wind pushed through the humid Texas air. David heard all of this, saw images passing by all around him, but the light of Anna's eyes seemed to outshine all of that. He was smitten, but he chalked it up to being home. Having such a reaction to the petite blonde would be normal for any man who'd been at war, he supposed. She was easy on the eyes.

David had dreaded this journey. Finally, things were looking up. While everyone around him celebrated Ali's safe entry into the United States, David thought back over the last forty-eight hours and the intensity of his final mission as he'd airlifted Ali away from Camp Die-Hard to a staging area and on to Landstuhl, Germany, to a waiting C-17 air force plane.

Now that David had made it home to Texas, he stood back as he always had, watching. He'd grown up in Prairie Springs, but he had never been a part of this place. He'd been a struggling outsider back then, and now his worst fear was that he'd return to that yet again—no matter what he'd done to serve his country. And no matter how interested he was in the pretty blonde who'd started this whole chain of events.

But they weren't the only two who'd worked to get this little boy to America and safety. Ali's grandfather had called in a whole passel of favors, though still making sure he went by the letter of the law to get the little boy to Texas. The old warhorse had finally realized he'd failed his son, but Ali would give all of them a renewed chance to make things right. To honor the memory of Greg and Karima Willis.

David prayed they'd be able to help the lost little boy both physically and spiritually.

His gaze held Anna's, and he wondered if she was praying for the very same thing.

"We need to tell Dr. Blake about Ali's cough. With all the cameras and press, I didn't get a chance to brief her when we came in."

Anna looked away from David to find army nurse Maddie Bright tugging at her arm. "I can't get her attention," Maddie said.

Anna turned back to David with a reluctant shrug. "Excuse us, please."

He gave her that soldier nod she'd become so familiar with over the years of working closely with Fort Bonnell personnel. "Go on. I'll be right here," David said.

That drawling promise sent a foreign tingle down Anna's spine. The pilot was certainly good-looking, but the man had been through the worst of the war. He'd be hungry for any sort of feminine attention. Even hers.

Putting her mind back on Ali's needs, she escorted Maddie to where Dr. Nora Blake loomed over the boy, checking his vitals while she ignored the reporters trying to get her attention.

Anna pushed through the crowd. "Dr. Blake, this is Madeline Bright, the nurse who accompanied Ali home. She needs to speak to you."

"Talk," the blond, no-nonsense doctor ordered without even glancing up.

"I'm worried about fluid backing up into his lungs." Maddie hurriedly explained that both she and the on-board flight nurse had monitored Ali during the long, grueling trip across three continents.

Dr. Blake stood silent, allowing Maddie to vent her worries then said, "Dr. Montgomery explained some of that in his last report. He said Ali's ankles and feet have been swollen. That's why we pushed so hard to get him here as quickly as possible."

Maddie nodded. "Swelling's not a good sign."

Dr. Blake glanced over Ali's charts. "No, it is not. We'll check that and probably put him on digoxin to help his heart pump and lasix to get rid of the fluid. We need to get him in tip-top shape before we even attempt the surgery." Snapping the chart shut, she stood straight again. "Does that ease your mind?"

"Yes, ma'am," Maddie said, relief evident in her sigh. "Thank you."

"She's a good nurse," David said as he moved closer to Ali's stretcher.

"I'm glad you both got permission to accompany Ali," Anna replied, liking his soft smile. "It's so horrible to think he lost both parents in this war."

David nodded, his eyes going dark. "That's why we wanted to get him to his grandfather. They have only each other now."

"Well, thanks again," Anna said. "You're a local hero now."

He balked at that. "No, ma'am. I'm just a soldier, doing my job."

Anna let it go at that, since she'd brushed off his earlier compliment to her. She was happy to see Ali surrounded by people who cared about him so much.

But she couldn't help thinking about the man who had escorted Ali home and what little he'd told her about Karima's death and Ali's injuries. She longed to hear more about his war experiences, but she also knew the pilot would need some time. Readjustment to post life could be very stressful for any returning soldier. Anna hadn't known David before he left right after high school to train to be a pilot, but she'd heard that he'd requested a Permanent Change of Station so he could come back to Fort Bonnell to finish out the two remaining years of his current enlistment. Sending him a covert glance, she decided she'd like to get to know him now, though, when and if he was ready for a friend.

She had so many questions, and not all of them pertained to the war. She wanted to understand the kind of man who'd go out of his way to help an in-jured child. The kind of man who, much like her own deceased father, was willing to lay down his life for his brother. The kind of man who could bring life coursing back through her numb system simply by looking at her.

But Anna's questions would have to remain silent. Right now, everyone who had been so instrumental in getting Ali to Texas was here to welcome the tiny, obviously scared five-year-old to the United States. After this quick greeting, Ali would head on up the hall for testing and observation, so that Dr. Blake could get him ready for surgery in a few weeks.

Anna did plan to thank David again in a more formal setting for all his help in getting Ali here. And she hoped David would open up to her about more than just the little boy. Because from the way he stood to one side, silent and somewhat unsure, Anna had a feeling David *could* use a friend now that he was back on post. Maybe she was just imagining the way his dark eyes gleamed with interest every time he looked at her. But, every time he looked at her, he was smiling.

Chapter Two

David stood watching as the hospital staff prepared to wheel Ali away. Dr. Nora Blake marched behind Ali's stretcher, her hands up to keep people from crowding in too close, her expression as chilly as a cold desert night.

Ignoring the loud questions from a group of local television and radio reporters who'd followed them from the airfield, she shouted, "Okay, people. Let's finish so Ali can get settled in for some tests and some quiet time before he goes home in a couple of days."

David got the distinct impression nobody messed with Dr. Nora. She looked as intense as a colonel about to lead his troops into battle. She seemed to soften when she looked down at Ali, but the coolness was still there in her stance, just the same.

David could understand that intensity. He'd felt that way for the last two days, his mood waffling between worry for Ali and relief that they were going home. Now that Ali was here, David had fulfilled his duty. His part of this important mission was over. All he could do now was pray for the scared little boy and hope Ali adjusted to his new life in America. And that the surgery to repair his heart would be successful.

But what now for me? he wondered. Life stateside was always jarringly surreal after being in the thick of things for months on end. He'd have to take a few days of his R & R to get acclimated to his home town and to Fort Bonnell again. He had over a couple of months leave, but he wasn't sure what he'd do with that time. His mother wanted him to come visit her in Louisiana, but David wasn't quite ready for that trip. Not yet.

Anna held Ali's hand, then leaned close. "We'll all be right here, Ali. You're home now. You're safe."

Chaplain Steve added his own words to that, but in Arabic. Ali beamed a smile in return, then gave the chaplain a weak high-five. "Safe. A-mer-ica."

A woman who'd been introduced as Julia Saunders stepped forward. "Dr. Blake, remember, if you need me—"

"Thank you, Julia. We'll see how Ali handles being in America, but if we need a consult, you'll be the first to hear."

David strolled over to wave to Ali then gave Anna a questioning look. "What kind of consult?"

"Julia is a social worker. She often helps Children of the Day and was involved in helping us bring Ali over," Anna explained. "She's very interested in Ali's case and his adjustment to life over here. He'll be living with his grandfather and guardian, General Willis."

David nodded. "Dr. Mike went beyond the call of duty to get him here."

"Can you tell me more about what happened?" Anna asked. "It must have been awful for Ali, losing his mother and being all alone." Then she shook her head. "I'm sorry. You might not be ready to talk about that."

"It was a bad day," David said, memories of dust and death and the roar of choppers always nearby. He hadn't talked to anyone, not even his friend Maddie, about the day Ali came into the CASH, but he felt strongly that he could trust Anna, that she would understand. So he took her aside and started telling her in a quiet voice, reliving each second of that dark, dust-covered day. "Major Mike Montgomery— Dr. Mike—called me to the CASH with bad news. I figured we'd lost another soldier."

Anna nodded sympathetically.

"I was tired and ready to hit the sack. We'd had a grueling day transporting the wounded, but when he told me it was Karima and Ali, well, I got over there as fast as I could."

Anna touched a hand to his arm. "We heard it was a bomb."

"She was bringing him in for a checkup. Their vehicle got hit by an IED—an improvised explosive device—about five miles from camp. Karima was killed instantly and Ali was in bad shape."

David remembered rushing across the sprawling

tent city and into the camp hospital, adrenaline and shock pushing away his fatigue. "I couldn't believe it. Karima and Greg Willis fell in love in spite of the odds. Greg fell for her the first time she came into camp."

"She was a vital part of our organization over there," Anna said, tears welling in her eyes. "And I know she loved Greg and Ali so much."

David nodded, wondering what that kind of love would feel like. He'd never had that, not even from his mother and certainly not from his father. "He married her even though General Willis disowned him for it. After Greg's chopper went down, Dr. Mike and I vowed to watch over Karima and little Ali."

"From what I've heard, you did exactly that," Anna replied, her tone low but sure, her pretty eyes full of compassion.

David basked in her look and immediately started feeling better about things. "We failed him," he said. His prayers for little Ali had been front and center in his mind as he'd headed into the chaos of the surgical field hospital. "He looked so fragile and pale. But Dr. Mike and Maddie worked hard to get him stable."

Anna listened to his story, her gaze holding his as if he were the only person in the busy waiting room. "I'm so glad Ali had the two of you. Thank you again for helping us. I know his grandfather will appreciate it."

David nodded, feeling humble all over again. "It was my last mission—to get Ali here. I'm glad I did."

Dr. Mike had explained that the trauma of the boy's injuries had created a hole between the lower chambers of his heart and it could only be repaired by someone who was highly skilled. According to Mike, Dr. Nora Blake was one of the best cardio surgeons in the country. She lived in Prairie Springs and worked in dual capacity at both the Fort Bonnell Medical Center and at a large urban hospital in nearby Austin. Dr. Mike trusted her with Ali's life.

And apparently, so had Ali's paternal grandfather.

David glanced over at the crowd watching and waving to the little boy. "I hear even old Warhorse Willis himself is softening. Guess it's true if the boy's going to live with the old man."

Anna gave him a measured look, the slight disapproval of his choice of labels disappearing from her eyes in a twinkle. "General Willis has come a long way in letting go some of his preconceived notions, yes. He's invested more than just money in Ali's care and well-being, I think. This little boy has given General Willis a new lease on life." She glanced out the double glass doors. "In fact, he's supposed to be here today."

David wondered if the ornery old general would show. When he used to complain about never knowing his father, Greg would tell him that might be a blessing in disguise. General Willis had been tough on his only son, demanding that Gregory follow in his footsteps by joining the army. Greg had been good at what he did, a real hero, but he'd angered his father by enlisting straight out of high school rather than going to officer's training school as the general had planned. Things had gone downhill in the relationship from there on. Two different men, two different mindsets about war. At least Greg had had someone to fight against. Someone to fight *with*. It was one thing to fight strangers in a war, but another to have family with which to fight…and love and laugh. That kind of intimate relationship, no matter good or bad, was important.

As if thinking of the general had conjured him up, the doors swished open and in walked retired Brigadier General Marlon Willis. David noted how much the general had aged, but the man still carried himself like a soldier. Even with leathery lines slashing his face and a distinct slowness to his gait, the general demanded respect. David gave it to him with a salute.

"At ease, soldier," the general said with a returning salute and a wry smile, his custom-made cowboy hat in his hand as he read David's name tag. "Chief Ryland, it's good to see you home safe and sound." Then the tall, white-haired man turned to where Ali still sat on the stretcher. Glancing down at the boy, the general stood silent for a minute, then looked over at Anna. "Is this my…grandson?"

David watched as Anna touched a hand to General Willis' shirtsleeve. "Yes, sir. This is Ali."

The boy stared up at his grandfather with awe and fear, then looked toward his friend Chaplain Steve, a man he trusted since he and Steve had been e-mailing each other through Dr. Mike.

Steve leaned close. "Grandfather," he said, pointing to Marlon.

Ali grinned, his limited English enough to under-stand one of the words Steve and Dr. Mike had tried to teach him. "Grand…father," he said, the one word long and drawn out. Then he grinned. "Grandpa."

Marlon grunted, but David didn't miss the mist covering the old man's steely eyes. "Hello, there, young fellow. I've hired a very nice nurse to help us. I figure we'll both benefit from that."

David and Anna laughed at the general's wry humor.

Marlon nodded to everyone, then turned to Dr. Nora. "Tell me everything, doc. And I mean, everything."

"Let's get Ali into his room and get some tests going, then we'll go into my office," the doctor said.

Marlon nodded then took one of Ali's tiny scarred hands. "It's you and me now, kid. Two cowboys fighting off the bad guys."

Ali nodded back. "Cowboy. Yippee!"

"I see someone has been teaching you how to be-come a Texan," the general said with a smile.

David felt as if his world had shifted. Seeing Ali and his grandfather connect for the first time brought back the bitterness he'd felt for so long against his own absent father. And made him miss Gregory and Karima with an aching clarity.

Not wanting to be morose and bitter on this day of celebration, David glanced at Anna. As if sensing his eyes on her, she turned. "Chief, would you like to go get some breakfast with us?"

David looked around. Most of the others had left, even the eager reporters hoping for a heartwarming homecoming sound bite or a gut-wrenching picture for the front page. Maybe it was time for him to do the same. After all, he didn't have anyone waiting to welcome him home. He'd told his mother to stay in Louisiana, that he'd call her the minute he landed. And he'd gotten that uncomfortable call out of the way earlier, thank goodness. The only thing on his agenda for the next week or so would be the mandatory post-deployment training that all the returning troops had to go through.

When he saw Chaplain Steve's assessing gaze, he shook his head. "Another time maybe. As the chaplain knows, I have to go through a PDHRA before I can be considered human again."

Steve grinned. "You look human enough, Chief, even if you are wearing ACUs. But yes, I expect I'll be seeing you for part of your reintegration process this week. Still…you don't have to get started on that right away. Sure you don't want to come to breakfast with us?"

The challenging look in Anna's eyes made him wish he hadn't been so hasty in saying no.

David thought about his options.

"Let me see," he said, scratching his head. "Post deployment health assessment, or breakfast—a real breakfast—with people who aren't in a big hurry to get to the fight. Hmm."

Anna lifted her head. "Oh, we're always in a hurry around here, but we just take our time getting there."

That brought a smile to his face. "Then I guess I

might as well start my debriefing with a big Tex-Mex omelet and some real coffee."

"I know just the place for that," Caitlyn said, her arm linked in Steve's. "You remember Prairie Springs Café, right, David?"

David laughed. "Is Max still there?"

"Still there," Anna said as she motioned him toward the door. "And if I know Max, he'll pull out the red carpet for a returning hero. Might even give you a free meal." Tossing him a smile over her shoulder, she said, "Welcome home, cowboy."

Anna watched as David wolfed down the last of his big omelet, then reached for another biscuit. "Did you miss American food, Chief?"

David buttered the flaky biscuit, then put down his knife. "It wasn't so bad. We had something very close to American food on most days. That and our MREs, of course."

Caitlyn wiped jelly off one of the twins' mouths. "But a ready-to-eat meal can't take the place of the real thing, can it?"

"No, I reckon not," David replied, noticing the way Caitlyn and the chaplain kept smiling at each other. "You two an item or something?"

Steve burst out laughing. "You don't mince words, do you?"

Embarrassed, David shook his head. "I guess I don't. I believe in being up front and honest. But I can be too blunt at times, or so I've been told."

Anna looked down at her plate, thinking she believed in honesty herself. They had that in common at least. She didn't even know David Ryland…but she sure knew *of* him. He was considered one of the finest medevac chopper pilots at Camp Die-Hard. Or so she'd heard. Dr. Mike couldn't say enough nice things about him. The devoted doctor had called in several markers just so David could be the one to get Ali safely home. And yet, he'd asked Anna to watch over his friend David, too.

"Take care of him for me, Anna. He's a good man. But he's not so forthcoming about himself. Maybe you can draw him out, make him feel welcome."

Dr. Mike's words came back to her now as she glanced up at David. "Are you glad to be home?"

He nodded, his dark eyes washing over her intensely. "I guess I am. Time will tell."

Curious about that remark, Anna was about to ask him why he wasn't more excited, but the jingling bells on the café door caused her to stop and look up. "Uh-oh."

David turned to stare at the attractive older woman entering the café, then glanced back at Anna. "Is something wrong?"

Anna lowered her head, her hand going to her necklace. "No, nothing I can't handle. My mother just walked in."

Max waved a beefy hand from behind the counter. "As I live and breathe, if it ain't one of my favorite people. How ya doin', Olga?"

Olga waved back to Max, her smile somewhere between shy and coy. "I'm just fine, thank you."

"That's your mother?"

Hearing the surprise in David's words, Anna could only nod. "Yes. Olga Terenkov in the flesh. Get ready."

"Okay," David said, noticing the amused expressions on Caitlyn's and Steve's faces. "Should I be worried? I mean, she looks harmless."

That brought a grunt from Steve and a snicker from Caitlyn. But the twins seemed happy to see Anna's mother. They squealed and waved, calling out, "Miss Olga, Miss Olga!"

The woman waved back, clearly glad to see the cute little girls. "Hello, my darlings!"

"*Harmless* is not a word I'd associate with my mother," Anna said under her breath. "She's been doing things to embarrass me for most of my life and I have a feeling that's not going to change anytime soon."

Steve leaned close, his eyes on David. "Be forewarned, David. You're about to enter the hug zone."

David did look worried now. "But I—"

"Anna!"

Anna cringed. "We're in for it." She sent her beaming mother a feeble wave. "Hello, Mother."

Olga, still young looking at fifty-four, was dressed in her usual get-up—brown cowboy boots and a denim prairie skirt with a crisp flower-sprinkled cotton blouse. Her golden-blond hair was pulled up in a haphazard coil.

"Anna-bug," Olga called out, the click of her boots

hitting the hardwood floor as she sashayed up the aisle, "I've been looking everywhere for you. Isn't little Ali just adorable? Can you believe he's finally here? Did you get to give him a hug? Is he terribly afraid? Oh, I can't wait to see him again."

By this time, Olga was standing at the table, her mouth poised for yet another rapid-fire question when she stopped in midbreath to pin David with a wide-eyed appraisal. "Oh, my. And who are you?"

David stood, out of respect, but hesitated, caught in midair as if he wasn't sure what to do next. "Hello, ma'am."

Olga held a hand to her face, then giggled. "So polite."

"Mother, this is Chief David Ryland," Anna said, hoping the telltale hives she usually got along her jawline and neck whenever she was embarrassed wouldn't show up today. "He's the helicopter pilot who flew Ali to meet the C-17 to Germany. He escorted Ali home."

Olga put a hand to her heart, then touched it to David's sleeve. "Oh, oh, my goodness, we are so very thankful for you. So very thankful."

Anna noted her mother's Russian accent thickening. Olga's accent always came out whenever she was excited, and that was just about every day. Her mother was such an optimist, always looking on the bright side of things. And right now she had her sights set on David Ryland, which meant she was looking at the bright side of her daughter having breakfast with a returning soldier. When Olga glanced from David to Anna, her big blue eyes full of that hopeful glimmer Anna both admired and dreaded, Anna knew that two things were about to happen.

Olga put a hand on her hip, then looked up at David again. "Did you have anyone waiting at the airfield for you, son?"

David shook his head. "Well, no, ma'am—"

David didn't get to finish. He was immediately engulfed in a feminine hug and a whole lot of patting on the back. "Bless your heart. Bless you," Olga said over and over, her smile turned toward Anna as she looked over David's broad shoulder. "We're so glad you made it home safely with our little Ali!"

Caitlyn and Steve sat back, observing, grins covering their faces. Even the twins stopped eating to stare up at Olga.

Anna saw her mother's mirthful wink. Notorious for her outlandish matchmaking schemes, Olga would try to fix up David Ryland with her daughter. And that meant Anna's already chaotic life had just become even more complicated.

Chapter Three

Two days later, David sat in Chaplain Steve's office. After having gone through hours of being poked and prodded, questioned and tested, he was now waiting for the required assessment by the chaplain, just to make sure his spiritual health and well-being was intact.

"And I guess that's where the chaplain comes in mighty handy," David said out loud.

The door opened and Steve walked in with a smile on his face. "If you're talking to yourself, you might not pass all those tests you've been going through, my friend."

David laughed, then shook Steve's hand. "Don't worry, I'm not having a post-traumatic-stress moment."

"That's good," Steve said as he sank down in the squeaky chair behind his desk. "But you know whatever you say to me is strictly between us. So you don't have to pretend. How are you, really?"

David shrugged. "I've caught up on my sleep and

I've settled into my lovely post apartment. Well, I've got a wide-screen television and a big recliner and a bed at least."

Steve laughed at that. "What are your plans for the future?"

"For the immediate future? Getting accustomed to being reassigned to Fort Bonnell, for starters. Being a warrant officer on post is not nearly as demanding and exciting as being up in my chopper on the front. I'll be pushing papers for the next two years. Life here is sure a lot slower. I still can't get the sound of choppers and gunfire out of my mind, but it's good to be home."

"So what *are* your plans for...after?"

David leaned back, comfortable to be talking about anything but his spiritual well-being. "You know, I haven't mapped that out. But I wouldn't mind working as an EMS pilot for one of the nearby medical centers. I'd still pilot a chopper and I'd be able to help save people, but I won't get shot at—a definite plus for that kind of work."

"Always a good and noble career choice, too," Steve said. "They'd be blessed to have you."

"We'll see when the time comes," David replied.

Steve kept tapping his pen against his notepad. "What about right now?"

David glanced around. "You mean, what am I doing with myself these days? Everyone keeps asking me that and I'm not sure. I've been away for a long time now. For some reason, it just seemed important to come here before I take an official leave." Maybe because he had something to prove, even now. Or maybe because he was determined to find out who his father was.

They talked a few more minutes then Steve said, "You know, Children of the Day can always use good volunteers. There's a need for carpentry, painting, putting things together, taking things apart. Or just doing paperwork, making phone calls and packing care boxes for the troops. You might ask Anna and her mother about the possibilities."

"I might," David said, smiling as he shook his head. "That Olga is quite a character, isn't she?"

"She sure is. She has these wild schemes for setting up singles at church. Some of the members frown on her methods, but Olga is a very dedicated Christian. She means well."

David wondered about that and about Olga Terenkov. "Why hasn't she ever remarried?" And why wasn't her lovely daughter married?

Steve laughed out loud. "Probably because she intimidates every man she meets. Rumor has it she's got her eye on Reverend Fields. That would certainly be an interesting match." Then he tapped his pen again. "Don't go spreading that. I shouldn't be gossiping about Anna's mother."

David nodded. "I don't spread gossip. I know how it feels to be talked about."

Steve homed in on that revealing remark. "Did you have a good childhood, growing up here?"

Oh, boy. Now he'd have to go through all the angst from his past. "Yep." He shrugged, unable to hide the truth from Steve. "Well, no. Not all good. I didn't go without food or clothes, but it was tough. My mother…she was a single mom. She was stationed here before I was born and somehow even after her time serving at Fort Bonnell was up, we stayed."

Steve dropped his pen then moved on. "How's your faith?"

David looked down at his hands. "It's still intact. More than ever, I believe. But…I do need to work on it a bit. I mean, there's frontline faith and then there's that kind of pure faith on a Sunday morning coming down. There's a country song about that, in fact."

Steve nodded. "I know that song. Written from the heart. But you don't have to sit outside the church doors, my friend. God wants you to come on in." Then he stood up. "I think you're on the right track, David. But I encourage you to go see Anna. She could use some help."

"I'll keep that in mind," David said. "Working with Anna wouldn't be so bad."

Steve grinned. "She's a great person. And so is her mother. Maybe you can replace some of those bad memories from your past with some good ones." Then he shook David's hand. "Just remember, if you need anything—"

"I know where you are," David replied. "And…I do appreciate your help and the suggestion about volunteering. I'll see what I can do."

"I think you'd be an asset and I know Anna could use the help. She works very hard."

David couldn't deny that. "Children of the Day has been a constant presence during this war. Maybe it is time I give 'em some payback."

"Only if your heart is in it," Steve cautioned.

David nodded, then left the quiet office. His heart would be completely involved in helping others, but he wondered how it would react to being around Anna. It did seem to speed up whenever he was with the pretty blonde. And that was cause for both wonder and worry.

Anna sat in the swing on the wraparound porch of the rambling Victorian house where she worked and lived. The COTD offices took up the first floor while Anna and Olga had a spacious apartment on the second.

Today her mind was centered on the charity's latest hard-fought cause, bringing Ali to America. Children of the Day worked diligently to help anyone suffering from the damage and destruction of war, and her whole team had done their best to help General Willis get Ali Tabiz to Texas. Now she could rest easy knowing the little boy would be taken care of. And he'd have a chance now—a real chance to grow and thrive. Anna just hoped General Willis would keep opening his heart toward the boy. They needed each other.

She had taken a rare moment to come and sit in

one of her favorite spots so she could regroup and prepare for another busy workday tomorrow. This was one of her spots to pray. It gave her a good view of the tree-lined streets and the world beyond the busy Veterans Boulevard, yet she felt protected and cocooned here on the wide, deep porch, surrounded by towering magnolias and pines and lush crape myrtles. She could rock the swing back and forth and talk to God, calming herself after a long day.

But tomorrow should be a good day even if it was going to be shipment day. That always involved packing boxes full of supplies for the soldiers and emergency relief packages for the villagers. It always amazed her how many generous people brought things for those boxes. And some of the requests were interesting—anything from paperclips to toothpicks and bug spray or Bibles, books and candy bars. But Anna got the soldiers what they needed, one way or another.

Now that everything was in place with Ali and every precaution had been taken—all the proper paperwork had been filed and all the necessary steps of getting through government red tape had been carefully taken care of—Anna could get back to the day-to-day operations of COTD.

Thank You, Lord. Anna rocked back and forth on the white swing, her mind whirling with relief. She'd helped to save a child from war, but she didn't want Ali to be afraid about the surgery. Because Anna herself remembered being little and afraid because of war.

She was about to get up and finish some work before her mother came home for dinner when she heard a truck idling out on the street.

Surprised that anyone would be stopping by this late in the day, she held her foot on the floor to halt the swing. When David Ryland got out of the truck, Anna gulped in a breath to hide her shock.

"Hello," she called, waving to him as he walked up the steps.

"Hello, yourself," he said in response. Then he slipped his hands into the pockets of his jeans, staying on the steps while he surveyed the house. "Impressive."

Anna got up, too nervous to sit still. "The house was built around the turn of the century—1901 I think. My mother knows the entire history of this place."

He nodded then glanced out at the old oaks and tall pines. "So this is where you live and work."

"Yes." She nodded, her hands clasped in front of her. "So what brings you to see us today anyway?"

He grinned then scratched his thick short hair. "I guess I'm here to volunteer. At least, that's what Chaplain Steve suggested this morning."

"You don't look so sure," Anna replied. In fact, he looked downright uncomfortable.

"Oh, I don't mind volunteering," he said. "It's just that…well…I've been on the front for so long, I guess I've forgotten how to talk to a woman."

Anna chuckled, hoping to hide the blush moving down her face. "But you were around women in combat, right?"

"Uh, right. Whole different kind of thing." He shrugged. "It's been a very long time since I've seen a pretty woman sitting in a swing on a summer night."

"Oh, I see." Anna liked the way he drawled out his words. Then she said something that surprised them both. "You're welcome to sit here with me for a while."

"That would be nice," he said, motioning to the swing. "But don't let me keep you."

"No, it's okay. I was taking a break before I go back in to finish up some things."

He let her settle into the swing then sat down beside her, his weight shifting the creaky chains. Anna thought how different it felt, having someone beside her in this old swing. Different and a bit disconcerting, considering how her mind went into sensory overdrive with this man. She noticed the fine hairs on his forearms, the soapy clean scent surrounding him. And she noticed how he kept giving her an almost shy smile.

"So where do I sign up?" he asked.

"How good are you with a hammer and nails, Chief?"

David gave her a deadpan look then said, "Well, ma'am, It's been a while but I think I remember how to swing a hammer. But I might hit my thumb instead if you smile at me and distract me."

Anna's blush reheated. "I'll take that as a yes."

He nodded, laughing. "I'll do whatever you need me to do around here. I just need to stay busy."

She relaxed, and fought the temptation to fan herself. What on earth was wrong with her? She was acting like her mother. Never one for theatrics, Anna gave herself a serious reprimand and reminded herself she couldn't get involved with this man, for oh so many reasons. "I'll just take you out back to the playground. We're trying to rebuild it so it can be up to code. We'll have several volunteers coming in the morning to pack boxes and such, and I think you'll enjoy working on that type of project. And the back porch steps need repairing. If you don't mind."

He gave her one of those killer smiles. "Don't mind one bit. It'll be nice to be out in the open without having to worry about getting shot or blown up."

She slanted her head toward him. "I can show you what needs to be done right now, if you want."

"That's fine, as long as I'm not keeping you from something else. I mean, it is quitting time and I'm sure you have an after-hours life."

Anna had to laugh at that. "Oh, yes. Very exciting. I get to go upstairs and settle down with more paperwork."

"Do you ever just get away from this place and have fun?"

"Hmm, let me see." She pursed her lips. "It's been a while. But I did go for ice cream with some of my coworkers last week."

"I like ice cream. Maybe I can help in that department," he said, the gleam in his eyes enticing.

"Uh, about that playground—" She got up to find some breathing room. Turning she said, "If you'll just follow me."

She didn't miss the appreciative look he gave her. "So what exactly goes on around here?" he asked as they walked inside into the cool, dark hallway of the old house. "I know all about what your organization does, but what actually goes on back here?"

She turned at the porch door and said, "Oh, all kinds of things. We gather supplies to send to the war, we keep clothing on hand to give to the families of the soldiers and to give to those in other countries who are affected by the war, and well…we do whatever we can to help the children, including letting some of them live here temporarily if need be until relatives or foster care can take them in. They're our main concern. Some of them become neglected, even though they still have a parent here. The stress of being a single parent with a spouse overseas becomes too much for some. We try to help with that, too."

David held the door open for her then squinted toward the setting sun. "I guess I was lucky that way, at least. My mother was a soldier stationed at Fort Bonnell, but she always took care of me, somehow. But that's the thing about war. The children certainly suffer more than anyone else and they're so helpless."

"Yes, they are," she said, her mind whirling with a million questions about his childhood. "So you don't have any relatives close by?"

He looked down at the gray boards of the porch. "No, I don't. My mother moved to Louisiana and…I never knew my father."

"Oh, I'm sorry to hear that." She waited a beat

then gave him a direct look. "Then I guess you really do understand…about why Children of the Day is so important."

David nodded. "Oh, I understand, all right. That's why I took Chaplain Steve up on his suggestion and came here to volunteer. I know exactly what it's like to be little and afraid, and full of anger and questions."

Anna saw darkness in his eyes and wondered just how much this man had suffered. She'd lost her father when she was young, but David had never even known his. That kind of pain left a deep, cutting scar.

But it immediately endeared him to Anna and made her want to nurture him and help him to heal. After all, that was her job.

Chapter Four

Early the next morning Anna heard the whine of a sports car's gears shifting outside the house. Glancing up, she saw her best friend Trisha Morrison bringing her shiny white roadster to a grinding stop just inside the driveway. It didn't take Trisha long to make her way into the front lobby then straight into Anna's office, shutting the glass-paned door after her.

"Hi," Anna said, waving. Then she noticed Trisha's downcast look. Since Trisha was usually bubbly and outgoing, Anna knew something was wrong. "Trisha?"

Trisha burst into tears. "Anna, I need…"

Anna jumped up to come around the desk. "Trisha, what on earth's the matter? Did you break up with Nick again?"

Trisha tossed back her silky brown hair and sniffed, then wiped her brown eyes. "No, Nick and I are fine. It's about Daddy."

"Oh, honey, I'm sorry," Anna said, hugging Trisha close. "Of course, you're still grieving."

Trisha's father, a brigadier general and once the commander of Fort Bonnell, had died a few weeks ago. Trisha had taken it very hard, since her mother had died years earlier. The apple of her father's eye, Trisha had always been somewhat of a pampered princess. His death had left her a wealthy heiress who hadn't been making the best of choices lately, but Anna loved her friend in spite of that. She knew Trisha was still struggling with this loss.

"Come and sit down. You're just having a hard day, right? Do you need to talk to Mother?"

"I can't tell Miss Olga this," Trisha said on a sob. "Not yet. I haven't even told Nick. I…came straight to you."

Anna gripped Trisha's hand. "And you found me." While her vivacious mother was the grief counselor at Prairie Springs Christian Church, Anna often found herself taking over in that capacity, too, at Children of the Day. Seeing grief firsthand was one of the downsides of her charity work. But being able to help the spouses and children of soldiers more than made up for all the pain she had to witness. And right now, her best friend was clearly in pain.

"Want to tell *me* about it?"

Trisha nodded, tears still streaming down her face as she sank into an old leather office chair. "Yes. I need your advice. I got this today. Daddy's lawyer gave it to me."

Anna stared down at the crushed envelope in Trisha's hand. "What is it? Part of the will?"

Trisha waved the envelope in the air. "Oh, it's much more than that. It's…it's so hard to believe." Then she looked up at Anna, her voice quivering. "He has a son, Anna. My father had an affair with another woman before I was born."

"What?" Anna dropped down in the brown wicker chair beside Trisha, her heart thumping. Trisha was right; she couldn't believe this.

Commander Morrison had been like her own father, always so kind and understanding, especially when she and her widowed mother had moved to Texas from Russia over twenty years ago. The commander and Mrs. Morrison had helped Anna and Olga become acclimated to all things Texas. He'd invited them to church and made sure they didn't want for anything. He'd even invited Anna to one of Trisha's parties, which was how they became friends in the first place.

Anna couldn't think of a better, more honorable man than Commander Morrison. Or a more loyal friend than Trisha.

"Are you sure?" she asked Trisha, her hand tightening on the arm of her chair.

Trisha nodded. "Oh, yes. Daddy left this for me to open after his death. It's all right here, Anna." She held the envelope up, but didn't give it to Anna. "And you won't believe who my half brother is. You just won't believe it."

Anna swallowed back her own shock. "Are you sure you want me to know?"

"You need to know," Trisha replied. "You have to know. But you need to understand, the man has no idea, no idea at all, that we had the same father. He doesn't even know who his father was, according to this letter."

Anna felt sick at her stomach. "Trisha, you're scaring me. Just tell me, please."

Trisha leaned close, her words barely above a whisper. "My half brother just got home a few days ago. He's back at Fort Bonnell. He escorted Ali here." She gasped, clutched a hand to her mouth. "It's David, Anna. My brother's name is David Ryland. He's back but he doesn't know that my daddy was his father. Oh, Anna, I have no idea how I'm going to tell him."

Anna couldn't speak. Last night she'd enjoyed her visit with David. She'd even hoped… Well, no need to hope for things that were impossible. There was no hope for them once David heard this news. It would make things very uncomfortable for them since he would soon find out that Trish and she were best friends. "I don't know what to say."

Trisha shook her head. "Me, either. Maybe I'll just try to avoid him."

Then Anna let out a gasp. "That might not be so easy. He came by last night. Trisha, he volunteered to help out around here. Starting today."

Trisha jumped up out of her chair. "I can't be here

when he arrives. I'm not ready for that." Before Anna could stop her, she rushed out of the house, slamming the big front door behind her.

Anna looked at the stack of mail on her desk and let out a sigh. She felt sick to her stomach. The phones were ringing, she had mail to read and a meeting with her board of directors to update them on the budget for next year. She tried to block out Trisha's news.

"Why him, Lord?" she whispered as she took a sip of the herbal tea she always kept nearby. "Why David Ryland?"

And why was she suddenly caught in the middle of this drama? Caught between keeping a secret for her best friend and keeping the truth from the man she'd just met and had just a smidgen of interest in?

Probably just as well that I try to stay clear of David myself, she thought. When did she even have time for a serious relationship anyway? She'd given up on love, and her work had become her first love. But it would have been nice…so nice…to get to know David, maybe even in a romantic way. Anna had forgotten what romance was all about. But she couldn't possibly think along those terms now, not with this big secret standing between them. She'd promised Trisha she wouldn't tell anyone about David's parentage. And it was Trisha's place to tell him when the time came.

Caitlyn walked in, armed with files and records for

the meeting. "Hi, Anna." Dropping the files on Anna's cluttered desk, she sat down. "What's wrong?"

Anna couldn't divulge her worries about David and Trisha, or mention how he made her heart do strange things, so she told Caitlyn about the prayer request Olga had called to discuss a few minutes ago. One that concerned Caitlyn and her children.

"Whitney and John Harpswell still haven't answered their e-mails from Evan and it's been weeks now. The twins haven't heard anything from them recently, have they?"

She *was* worried about Whitney and John. She didn't have to pretend on that subject. The newlyweds were overseas doing their duty for their country, but according to Whitney's brother, Evan Paterson, no one had heard from them in a while. Caitlyn Villard was COTD's care coordinator since she'd moved back to Prairie Springs to raise her nieces after the deaths of her sister and brother-in-law in the war. She would want to keep close tabs on this situation, too.

Caitlyn sat down in the old chair across from Anna's desk. "No, and we've been worried, too, but their correspondence is somewhat sporadic at best."

"Evan says Whitney always gets back to him within a day or two, just to let him know she's safe."

Caitlyn bit her lip. "I've tried to keep this from the twins, but they'll start asking questions soon. Is there anything we can do?"

"I've called several people already," Anna said,

glad to be able to focus on this instead of her own recent upset. "I'm waiting to hear back, but the press has already gotten wind of it and they've been calling all morning, thinking I might have a connection over there. I can't give the press my liaisons over there. Too dangerous."

Anna put her hands together on her desk then dropped her head to say a prayer for their safety while Caitlyn added her own "Amen." While it wasn't unusual for soldiers to go weeks at a time without any letters or e-mails, depending on where they were located, this particular couple had been corresponding with Caitlyn's young nieces through the Adopt-a-Soldier program at Prairie Springs Christian Church.

Olga had suggested the twins participate since they'd lost their parents to the war. The little girls had had a hard time dealing with their parents' deaths, so Anna prayed they wouldn't have to go through yet another horrible grief.

"I hope we hear from them soon." Then she glanced up at Caitlyn. "I haven't had a chance to track down any of my sources to see what they've found."

"Let me do that for you," Caitlyn offered, taking the file Anna had been studying. "I'll get on it right now. Maybe Steve can help, too. We've both been so worried, anyway."

Anna crossed her arms over her chest. "It's horrible. I wish this war could just be over, but war is never really over. It just changes locations." She tried not to let her own bitterness show whenever she was dealing with the victims of war, but she couldn't help herself. Sometimes, it was just too much. Shaking off the negative attitude, she got up, letting her efficient secretary, Laura, answer the ringing phone. "And yet, we soldier on, right?"

"Right," Caitlyn said, standing. "Maybe I can find out something for us, at least."

As Caitlyn was heading back across the hall to her own office, Anna called, "Oh, by the way, we have a new volunteer coming in today to help with the playground construction. David Ryland."

"Oh, really?" Caitlyn's smug look only added to Anna's confusion and frustration. "He seems like a good person."

"He *is* nice," Anna replied. "And he's on leave, of course, so he wanted something to do."

"Or maybe he wanted to be around you some more," Caitlyn said, smiling.

Anna glanced around the lobby, glad to see no one was waiting there. "C'mon now, you know I'm much too busy for a relationship."

"Maybe that's about to change," Caitlyn replied.

Anna's phone rang just as Laura came running from the back of the house. Caitlyn winked then went back to her office.

"I've got it," Anna said, waving her secretary back to her desk tucked in a corner out in the hall and hurrying back to her own office.

It was Trisha. "I need to ask you something. Is the coast clear?"

"He's not here yet, if that's what you mean," Anna said, lowering her voice.

"Good. I'm outside."

Anna shook her head as Trisha came in, waved to Caitlyn and Laura, then entered the office and shut the door. Again.

"Okay." Anna sat down in her squeaky chair. "What?"

Trisha threw down her leather tote then sat across from Anna. "What's he like? My brother, I mean? You said you had a good visit with him last night."

Hearing Trisha call David her brother jarred Anna. "He's a good man," she said, careful to stay neutral on the subject in spite of the way the man made her heart flutter. "He cares about our country and he's very dedicated to his job. And he was so humble about bringing Ali to us."

Trisha twisted a silky strand of her long brown hair. "Humble is good. But surprising. My father was anything but."

"You're right on that account," Anna agreed. "Even though your father was always kind to me, I've seen him dress down soldiers many times over."

Trisha's eyes misted. "He was always sweet to me, though. Firm, but loving. I miss him so much." She pressed her knuckles down on the desk. "Does David…does he look like my daddy?"

Anna pursed her lips, David's tall, rugged form coming into her mind with a perfect clarity. "He's tall and muscular, with dark hair and eyes. Yes, I guess now that I think about it, he does have your father's smile. David has a very nice smile."

Trisha's eyebrows lifted at that. "Sounds as if you noticed a lot about him."

Anna sat up and started straightening the clutter on her desk. "Last night wasn't the first time I've talked to him. We did have breakfast together the other day after we saw Ali safely to the hospital, but Steve and Caitlyn brought the twins and ate with us," she replied, hoping her blush didn't give her away. "And I'm very observant. You know that."

Trisha's smile was indulgent. "Yes, I do know that. So…you think he's okay, then?"

"I think David is just fine. And I do wish you'd call him up and ask him to meet you. You need to tell him everything. I don't like knowing this and not telling him. Especially when he's due here at any minute."

"I'm trying to find the courage," Trisha admitted. "I want to meet him first, see how he reacts to me. That's why I came back, but first I wanted to talk to you again. He won't know who I am, really. But I'd like him to get to know me before I blurt out that I'm his sister."

Anna leaned forward on the old metal desk. "I think David could use some family here. He wasn't very forthcoming about his mother. I wonder about that relationship."

"Well, she lied to him his whole life. We don't know what she told him regarding his absent father. That has to hurt." Trisha thought for a moment. "I do know that my father left some sort of trust fund to help his mother with finances." She shook her head. "I can't imagine how much more hurt he's going to be when he finds out the truth."

"You're both hurt by this," Anna said, wishing she could ease that pain. "But I believe there is a reason for everything. David chose to come back here. It's an opportunity to make things right. You have to tell him the truth."

Trisha nodded. "I will, I promise. But not just yet."

Anna hugged her friend close. "But soon, okay?"

"Okay." Trisha turned to leave. "I'll go get us some fresh tea, so we can tackle these files then get on with the care-package drive. The other volunteers will be here soon and I want to be ready to roll." She stopped, glancing out the window. "And I'll stay clear of David for now. So don't mind me. I won't make a fuss."

"Good idea," Anna said. "And just to keep myself busy so I don't blurt anything out, I'll go into the boardroom and get the monthly reports distributed before the board members start arriving." Then she heard the squeaking old front door opening. Glancing out through the glass of her office door, she saw David standing a few feet away. "Oh, we have company."

Trisha's eyes grew wide as she turned to stare at the tall, dark-haired man who'd entered the central hallway of the rambling old mansion. "We sure do." She whirled back to Anna. "Is that—?"

Anna grasped her friend's arm, causing Trisha to

yelp in pain. "Sorry." She sent Trisha a look that told her friend to stay put. "Yes, that's him."

The man looked up then waved through the closed glass door, his smile widening. "Hello."

"Hello, Chief Ryland," Anna called, her fingers putting pressure on Trisha's elbow. "You're right on time."

Trisha inhaled a breath. Anna could feel the tension in her friend's stance, but she held steady to Trisha's arm while they waited for David to stroll across the hall and into Anna's office. "Actually, Chief Terenkov, I thought I was a little early. But I'm ready to get started on that playground."

Anna let go of Trisha then pushed at her always-falling-down hair. "Good. I'll just show you where everything is. We've ordered all the proper equipment and supplies."

David chuckled, clearly enjoying her discomfort. Then he looked over at Trisha. "Hi. I don't think we've met. I'm David Ryland."

Trisha shot Anna an anxious look, then suddenly remembered her manners. "Hi, I'm Trisha Morrison," she said, extending her hand. "It's nice to meet you. I mean, I've heard so much about you. Anna was just saying—"

"Trisha Morrison? Are you related to Commander Morrison?"

"He was my father," Trisha said, her head down. "He died last month."

David didn't look surprised. "We got the news.

I'm sorry." Then he put his hands on his hips. "I guess you don't remember me, huh?"

Trisha looked toward Anna for help, fear and dread evident in her eyes. "No, I'm afraid I don't. Should I?"

"Never mind," David said. "I was a senior in high school when you were a freshman. It was a long time ago."

Trisha held tightly to her files and her tote bag. "I—I'm glad you made it safely home, David."

"We are indeed thankful that you managed to get Ali here for his surgery," Anna said to change the subject. "We do appreciate it."

"Yes, we do," Trisha echoed. "Very much."

"Please, no more thanks." David gave them another quizzical look. "I wasn't the only one. A whole lot of people care about little Ali. It's hard for a child to have to grow up without a parent. And now he's lost both of his."

Trisha busied herself with gathering files. "I—I have to go get busy."

Anna gave her friend a sympathetic look. "Are you sure?"

"Yes, pretty sure," Trisha said, her eyes misting up again. "I—it was nice to meet you, Chief Ryland."

"Call me David," David said as Trisha rushed past him. Then he turned to Anna. "Was it something I said? I think I remember her from high school, but maybe I have the wrong girl. She was a lot younger than me."

Anna's heart went out to David and Trisha. Trying to find the right words, she replied, "You'll have to forgive Trisha if she doesn't remember. She's been trying to deal with her father's death and a whole lot of other things."

"General Davis Morrison was a real soldier's soldier. His daughter might not remember me, but I sure remember him, even before he became commanding officer. And even before I joined the army. I used to see him on the evening news."

Anna's heartbeat accelerated. Even their first names were similar. "So you knew him personally?"

David shook his head. "Oh, no, nothing like that. We didn't run in the same crowd of course. I knew *of* him. A regular legend in his own time."

"He was that, indeed," Anna said. "His death hit all of us very hard."

"I'm sorry to hear that. He was a good soldier."

"Yes, he was dedicated to his country and the army."

David nodded as he glanced across the hall to where Trisha was now talking to a woman who'd just come in. "I didn't mean to upset her."

Anna wished she could change the subject, but she had to be careful. Trisha was putting on a good show, but she knew her friend was just trying to avoid the issue. "She'll be all right. Her mother died a few years ago and now her father. She's feeling all alone and it's been hard for her to adjust."

"Wow, that is tough. Does she work here?"

"She volunteers here," Anna explained. "Trisha

inherited her father's estate, so she doesn't have to work for a living. She had just moved back from Dallas when it happened, so she hasn't taken the time to decide what to do with her life. But she helps out here a lot, and she is looking for something to fulfill her, I think." She nodded toward the door. "She's a whiz with fundraising, so I've put her in charge of our annual black-tie ball. I'll send you an invitation."

David scoffed. "I don't do black tie. But I can do just about anything else you need done around here. So…what do you say we get started?"

Anna let out a sigh of relief. If he stayed out back all day, he could avoid Trisha's overly curious stares.

"I'll take you out to the old garage where we have everything stored," she said.

David followed her out the door and down the long hall.

And Trisha stood at the door of Caitlyn's office, watching them all the way.

Chapter Five

"So I hear Ali is doing okay. Maddie told me she went by to see him the other day."

Anna smiled at the way David's eyes lit up whenever he mentioned Ali. She watched as he stacked fresh lumber against the porch railings. He'd brought it over earlier so he could get started on repairing the back steps. And, Anna thought thankfully, her mother, who usually hovered around and helped out as needed, was over at the grief center at Prairie Springs Church, probably flirting with the reverend.

David had survived his first couple of days working at COTD and so far so good. As long as she kept Trisha away from him, Anna thought she could juggle this situation, at least for the time being.

"Ali is doing great at adjusting," she said, thinking she couldn't ignore the man after all. "Dr. Blake is watching him closely. She doesn't want to do the surgery until she's sure he's strong enough for the operation. But it's a fine line—trying to get him in better health without waiting too long."

David nodded. "Mike told me it was tricky, but he also explained that getting Ali here to rest and regain his strength would help him to heal better after the surgery. That's why we worked so hard to make it happen. Ali wasn't safe where he was."

"That's true," Anna replied. Then after admiring his biceps each time he lifted a two-by-four, she handed him a bottle of water. "I'm going to drive over to the general's house later today and visit Ali."

David took a long drink then smiled over at her, his expression hopeful. "Hey, I might go with you. I mean, I miss the little fellow."

Anna shifted on her tennis shoes, unsure of how to react. David had been true to his word about volunteering and now he was here almost every afternoon, ready to do whatever needed doing. And there was always something. But Trisha worked at COTD two or three days a week, too. The constant strain of trying to work with both of them, yet keep her mouth shut about what she knew, was causing Anna a lot of sleepless nights.

When she didn't answer, David looked away in embarrassment. "I didn't mean to invite myself. I'm sorry."

"Oh, no, that's okay," she said, her skin heating up. Why did the man do that to her? Every time she heard his boots hitting the front porch, she got all flustered and flushed. That was so not like her. Her mother might be all gushy and wide-eyed these days around an available man, but Anna had other things to occupy her mind. But she really liked being around David. He was smart and easy to talk with. He didn't demand answers or need immediate assistance. He was just…David. Quiet and unassuming, interesting and very Texan. And it would do Ali a world of good to see a familiar face.

Besides, she'd promised Dr. Mike that she'd watch after his friend and she had to honor that promise, didn't she? "I don't mind you going with me, David, really, I don't. I'm just surprised that you'd want to. Surprised and touched," she quickly added. "I didn't realize how close you'd become to Ali."

He put down his tape measure then flexed his shoulders in a quick stretch. "Now, why would that surprise you? I cared about Ali's parents and I care about him. Greg was one of my best friends and Karima, well, she was very dedicated to helping the children over there. She worked tirelessly to save as many of them as she possibly could. That little boy has seen a lot of horrible things. I won't abandon him now that he's in the States."

The troubled look in his eyes made Anna's heart open with understanding. "It *is* hard to explain war to children. I lost my father when I was just becoming a teenager and I guess I never quite got over it."

"I sure never knew mine," David said, almost to himself. "He didn't care enough about my mother and me to stick around. And unfortunately, a lot of people back then knew I was illegitimate. That didn't win me friends during school. I just don't want Ali to suffer that way."

Anna watched as his expression turned grim, making him look weathered and aged. She could almost see the scars there in his eyes and on his suntanned skin.

"I'm sorry, David," she said, truly meaning it. At least she had known her father, had known the strong love of a parent for a child. And she still had her mother, too. She couldn't imagine growing up with that kind of guilt and stigma hanging over her head.

"Yeah, me, too. I'm really sorry." He went back to his measuring, his mood changing right along with the Texas weather. When he took the hammer and pounded it against a nail, Anna got the impression he was beating against all the shame inside his soul.

"It looks like rain," she said for want of anything better to say. She'd have to remember to avoid the subject of his parentage from now on. "Want to go around four? We can go visit Ali and see how that nurse the general hired is holding up."

"I hope that ornery old man hasn't scared the nurse away," David said. But he kept his eyes on his work, as if he were afraid of looking at her. Or seeing her look at him.

Wanting to make him smile again, Anna giggled. "Oh, I don't think so. My mother and Julia helped find the perfect nurse for General Willis and Ali. Tilda Reynolds is retired from twenty years in the army and five years as an RN, and from what I've heard, she's like a drill sergeant. She won't take any antics from the general, trust me."

David laughed and the sound delighted Anna. He had such a great laugh. That and his Texas drawl only added to his charm. "Your mama is one smart woman. That Olga, she's…uh…interesting."

Anna pushed at a curling strand of hair near her temple. "That's a very diplomatic way of describing her. She's always been a bit flamboyant, I'm afraid. My mother is outgoing and energetic." She shrugged. "While her daughter is just plain, quiet Anna."

"You are not plain," David said, his hammer held high in one hand as he centered a board against the fresh, new railing. "Far from it."

"Thanks." Anna didn't miss the way his dark eyes moved over her face while he drawled those words toward her. She felt another little shiver moving throughout her system, even though it was about ninety-three in the shade. "Well, I guess I'll go back inside and get some work done. Just come by my office in about an hour and we'll go and see Ali."

"Are you sure you want me to go with you?"

"I'm very sure," she said. And she was. David needed Ali as much as the little boy needed support. "He'll be so glad to see you."

He gave her another long look then said, "He likes brownies. We might want to pick some up."

"I'll see what I can do about that."

Anna bounced up the steps and rushed inside to

the cool darkness of the long hallway. Letting out a sigh, she shook her head. "Too much sun."

"Hmph," came a noise from the big combination dining room and boardroom just to the right. Trisha stood at the arched doorway, shaking her head, a look of concern on her face. "Anna, he's got a thing for you. And I think you feel the same way."

"Whatever are you talking about?" Anna asked as she whirled by her friend. "And since when have you stooped to listening in on my conversations?"

Trisha tossed back her hair, following Anna into the kitchen. "Since the man you're talking to just happens to be my—"

"Shh," Anna said, pointing to the porch. "Do you want him to hear?" While the noise from ringing phones and laughing children could drown out their hushed conversation, Anna worried that David would walk in on them.

Trisha shook her head. "Of course not. But I don't like the way he looks at you. You don't know him well enough for that." Then she put a hand over her mouth and whispered, "I did look him up in the high-school yearbook. He *was* a senior when I was a freshman. He played football, but I don't remember him even though I dated a lot of football players. Isn't that horrible?"

"You were younger," Anna said, shaking her head. "But he does seem to have a vague memory of you."

"He's not worried about me," Trisha said. "He's only got eyes for you. And if he had seen you in school, I think he would have remembered you. You need to be careful."

Anna laughed then put a hand to her mouth. "This coming from a woman who falls in love at first sight. By the way, how is Nick these days?"

"Don't change the subject," Trisha replied, her arms crossed over her blue cotton blouse. "Besides, Nick is history. He wasn't worth my time, but he did think he was worth my money."

"Oh, honey, *you* need to be more careful," Anna said, moving into the kitchen to tidy up from the day's activities. "I worry about you."

Caitlyn strolled into the kitchen, her hazel eyes bright. "Why are we worried about Trisha today?" she asked, an indulgent grin on her face as she prodded Trisha with a poke from her elbow. "What's the drama queen up to now?"

"She broke up with Nick," Anna said, glad to shift the subject from David.

"Oh, too bad," Caitlyn replied with real concern. "Are you all right?"

"I'm fine," Trisha said, giving them a mock frown. "Nick is so off my radar." She started putting away the punch and cookies they'd served to a few of the neighborhood children during snack time. "I'm staying busy planning the fund-raiser. I've set the date for Labor Day weekend. What do you think?"

"That's only a few weeks away," Anna replied as she put away plastic cups and napkins. "Think we can have everything arranged by then?"

Trisha pursed her lips. "I'm a Morrison, Anna. I get things done in this town. Besides, I know all the caterers personally."

"Don't remind me," Anna said on a teasing note. "Just do what you need to do and fill me in on the details. You know how much I hate fund-raising."

"Yes, but you love the necessary money it brings in," Trisha reminded her. "And…you will be there, of course."

"She will," Caitlyn promised. Then she grinned. "And I sure will. I'll actually have a date."

Trisha smiled. "You are so in love with the chaplain. I envy that."

Anna envied Caitlyn's newfound love, too. Caitlyn and Chaplain Steve made a great couple. "It's nice to see the two of you hitting it off."

"Back to the fund-raiser," Caitlyn said, all business again. "I suppose we all need to make a good showing, right? We should encourage all of the employees and volunteers to attend. It'll be such a fun night and for a good cause."

"Of course," Anna said. But she dreaded getting all dressed up to attend a glitzy function when she knew that somewhere across the world people were suffering and dying. And yet, it was for that very reason that she would go and mingle with the elite of Fort Bonnell and Prairie Springs. She needed funds to keep Children of the Day running, both for the children here who missed their parents and the children over there who didn't have parents anymore. "You both know I'll do whatever I need to do to get the job done. And if that means wearing a formal dress, then I'm there. And my mother will be there, too. She'll probably make the entire congregation at church attend, including Reverend Fields."

Caitlyn smiled. "Good." Then she slanted her head toward the sound of hammering outside, her eyes on Anna. "And this year *you* just might have a date to bring with you."

"David? I doubt that. He indicated he doesn't like fancy gatherings."

Trisha looked doubtful, but joined in, probably for Caitlyn's sake, since she couldn't protest without giving an explanation. But she shot Anna a warning look just the same. "He might change his tune if you're on his arm."

Anna loved that particular image, though she responded, "I don't think so. And besides, since my best friend doesn't approve—"

Caitlyn picked up on that. "Trisha? And why not? The man is gorgeous and available. What's not to approve?"

"It isn't that I don't approve," Trisha interrupted, giving Anna a fleeting look. "It's just that…well…I had you first. You're my friend. I don't want to lose you." Then she slanted her head. "Is that selfish of me?"

Caitlyn laughed. "You, selfish? Trisha, get real. You might be a shopaholic and a socialite and have bad judgment regarding men, but you're generous beyond a fault. I've never known you to be jealous of anyone else's happiness."

"Nor have I," Anna added, putting an arm around Trisha's slender shoulders. "No, you are not at all selfish. And you will never lose me as a friend. I promise you that."

Trisha watched as Caitlyn grabbed a cup of coffee then headed out the door. "I'll see y'all later. I've got tons of work to do before the day ends."

Anna waited until they were alone again before whispering to Trisha. "I can imagine how hard this is for you—seeing him here each day. But soon, Trisha, all of that will be behind you. I think David will love having a sister."

"If he can forgive me for my father's transgressions, that is."

"We have to hope and pray that he can. And that he won't hold it against me that I knew all of this."

"I've put you in an awkward situation, haven't I?"

"I'll deal with that. The important thing is for you to come clean and get to know your only close relative. I think you and David will be good for each other."

"We'll see," Trisha said, tapping her tan patent pump against the tiled floor. "I need a little more time, but it does help, being around him. Even if he's more interested in *you* than me. At least the man has good taste in women."

Anna braced herself. "He's going with me to visit Ali later. Is that okay?"

Trisha rolled her eyes. "Anna, I was just teasing about that, honestly. Even if I'm not quite ready to be friends with David, you certainly deserve someone. And I do think he's nice. And Caitlyn's right, he's also gorgeous. Must be those good Morrison genes."

"He's hurting, Trisha. And it breaks my heart to think about it. I do hope you and he can become friends. Friends and brother and sister. Then, neither of you will be alone."

Trisha shook her head. "I'm not ready yet. But I will bake some brownies for you to carry to Ali."

"You listened to our whole conversation, didn't you?"

Trisha slanted her brows, her gaze lifting toward the old whirling ceiling fan. "Not all of it. Just enough to know the man is interested in you. But how else am I supposed to get to know him?"

Anna couldn't argue with that. Trisha's reaction to David was a mixed bag of both joy and dread. Anna didn't want to muddy the waters by getting too close to the man. She was playing with fire, just thinking about David Ryland. The man was a soldier; he had the nomadic life that being in the military required. And she was settled and happy here in Prairie Springs, doing the work she loved. She'd dedicated her life to developing Children of the Day. She didn't have time for a relationship.

Even if David Ryland did seem to be interested in her.

But she couldn't help sneaking a look at him as he worked just outside her door. She went to the big kitchen window and glanced down, watching as he held the hammer to a piece of board and drove the nail into the wood with precision.

For the first time, Anna realized her own need to find someone to ease this constant ache inside her heart.

Chapter Six

General Marlon Willis lived in the historical part of Prairie Springs, a few short blocks from the Fort Bonnell main entrance gate. His elegant, enormous home wasn't very far off Veterans Boulevard, and it was just around the corner from Anna's house and offices.

David stopped his pickup on the oak-lined circular drive, taking in the two-storied house with the big sloping lawn. "Ali's life sure has changed. He went from living in dark, damaged apartments and army tents to this. He lived in fear all the time over there and now he has peace and quiet and someone to cater to his every need. It's almost too much for a little boy to comprehend. But he's fighting a different battle now, I guess."

Anna opened her door and hopped out, careful to hold on to Trisha's basket of brownies and the book she'd brought as she looked over at David. "All the more reason for us to help him adjust. Dr. Mike is still sending him e-mails and I've heard the general hired a language coach to help Ali with his English. He's safe now, David. We can be thankful for that, at least."

David didn't argue with that. "I am thankful. I'm praying that the surgery will work and Ali gets to stay here in America. It's hard to believe I won't ever be able to play a game of volleyball with Greg again or attend church services with Karima."

She sensed something in him as he stared up at the imposing house before getting out of the truck. "Were you and Gregory very close before you went into combat?"

He gave a little laugh. "Not growing up. He was the popular kid of a general who'd come to Fort Bonnell to finish out his career. And me…I was a bad kid from the other side of town. The not-so-pretty side. People like Trisha and Gregory didn't exactly invite people like me to their pool parties or country clubs."

"That's right," Anna said, waiting as he opened his door. "You mentioned you remembered Trisha from high school."

He walked around to shut Anna's door, then followed her up the stone walkway toward the imposing house. "I saw her around and I knew her dad was a big shot on post. She was a little pipsqueak in with the cheerleader pack. Some of the girls would flirt with me, but I didn't have anything to offer back then. So I mostly tried to stay out of everyone's way."

Anna wondered if he got teased because of not having money. "I bet you were cute in high school."

He lifted an eyebrow. "Too bad I didn't know you back then."

"I'm afraid I was too terrified to venture out very much when I first arrived, and even after Trisha and I got to know each other, I didn't really run with the popular kids. I mostly sat at home, reading books and making plans to join the Peace Corps."

"That explains it then," he said as they walked up the stone steps. "We were both hiding in plain sight, all around each other. Because I'm sure I would have noticed you."

That made Anna blush. Wanting to get back on a safe subject, she said, "Tell me about Gregory's wife."

David lowered his head. "Karima was very special. She read her Bible every day and she prayed for her son and her husband. In spite of the dangers, Greg brought her hope in the Lord, and now I want that same hope for her son."

"I'm glad she had Greg," Anna said. "Now the general has a second chance with his grandson. It's a wonderful day. And it's a sign of God's devotion. Even though Ali lost his parents, he's given his grandfather a new hope. I have to believe God had a hand in that."

"You might be right there," David said. He couldn't explain the workings of the Lord, but he did believe God had a plan for everyone. He only wished God would reveal what was in store for his own future. Right now, however, he could enjoy getting to know Anna a little better.

David liked her positive attitude. In fact, he liked pretty much everything about Anna. She had a way of making the harried, angst-ridden people who came to her for help feel much better about things. And David included himself in that number. Just being around her reinforced his faith in God and his dedication to his career. She was fighting a war of her own by trying to help those who needed her, by sending supplies to the battle zones and by trying to hold things together for those left behind. That was not an easy task, but Anna was more than up to the job. She whirled around the offices, always stopping to answer questions or comfort a child. She worked long hours, but she also took time to stop for anyone who needed her.

He watched her now as she knocked on the big white door of the general's house, a children's Bible storybook for Ali in one hand and the brownies in the other. She wore her cross necklace—she always had it on—and her standard white blouse with dark sensible pants. Today she had on a pair of flat shoes with little flowers etched in the brown leather. Her blond hair was partially caught up in that silver clip she wore a lot, but she'd left part of it down around her shoulders.

"What?"

David's gaze moved from Anna's soft hair to her inquisitive eyes. "What?"

"I asked first," she said with a grin. "You were staring at me. So what is it?"

"Oh, that." Since he had her attention and she actually looked a little off-kilter, he decided to see if his flirting techniques were still intact. "Nothing. I just…I like your hair, Chief. It's nice."

Anna touched a hand to her temple, her eyes going wide. "Well, thanks. I rarely remember to brush it."

"I like that about you, too," he blurted, glad that a uniformed housekeeper was opening the door. Now he was the one getting all flustered.

"Hi, Gladys," Anna said to the housekeeper, her tone full of mirth at his discomfort. "We're here to see Ali and the general. I believe they're expecting us."

The gray-haired woman nodded. "If you'll just follow me out to the veranda."

"Veranda?" David whispered. "Where I come from, we call that a porch."

"Shh." Anna giggled as they followed the woman through the dark, spacious house and out a set of wide French doors.

David noticed an expensive-looking cowboy hat dangling off a set of deer antlers in the den off to the right. The general's way of hanging his hat, obviously.

"They're right over there," the woman said, pointing to a long white wicker sofa and two matching chairs set against one of the walls. "The general is reading to Ali." Then she turned and whispered, "I think they're hiding from Nurse Tilda."

That made both Anna and David laugh. Anna held her hand to her mouth. "Is it that bad?"

The maid nodded. "But she's a very good nurse."

Then she waved her hand. "Go on over. I'll bring y'all something to drink while you start in on those brownies."

David guided Anna across the cool tiles of the porch, the sound of three whirling fans up on the beamed ceiling blending with the chirping of birds and the drone of bees out in the garden. Somewhere off in the yard, the water spilling from a fountain added to the sense of grace and serenity.

When the old general looked up, his eyes showed strain. "Hello, there," General Willis said, nodding to Anna and David. "Welcome." He pointed to the two chairs. "Have a seat."

Ali was down on the floor, playing with several model cars. When he saw David, the little boy got up and ran straight into his waiting arms.

"Hey, buddy," David said, his gaze meeting Anna's. Holding the skinny kid close only reminded him of how much he missed his friend Greg. "How are you?"

Ali's smile was bright with hope and his eyes had lost that scared, sick look David remembered. "Good," Ali said, his English still unsure. "Very good."

The general laughed. "His English is getting better."

Anna touched a hand to Ali's arm. "Hello, Ali. Remember me? I'm Anna."

Ali gave her a shy smile. "Anna." He said the name slowly, but he smiled after he managed to get the word out. "An-na," he said again, grinning.

"That's right," Anna said. "You're doing great."

"Gr-eat," Ali replied, smiling again. Then he went over to where his grandfather sat.

Marlon patted the floral cushion and pulled the boy up against his plaid shirt. "Took us a while to get to know each other, but we're managing. We're quite a pair, don't you think?"

David looked from the boy to his grandfather. "It's good to see you two together, sir."

Marlon looked down at Ali. "I never dreamed…I never knew I'd be able to see my son in this boy. But Greg's image is there each time Ali smiles. And that has done my old heart good." Then he lifted his chin and said in a low voice. "We've both had a few nightmares. Nurse Tilda tries to comfort the boy, but we've found that if I can just hug him tight for a few minutes, he goes back to sleep without too much fuss."

David remembered how Karima had held her son tightly after Greg's death. The things this little boy had endured would probably do in most grown men. "I'm glad he has you, sir," David said, meaning it. He wanted to add that he was glad the general had his grandson, too, but he didn't want to overstep his bounds.

"What's the news on the surgery?" Anna asked, her smile reassuring as she looked at Ali.

Marlon's arm tightened on the boy. "Dr. Blake is hoping to fatten him up. Our nurse makes sure he's on a good, nutritional diet and she administers his medication every day. And mine, too, I might add. A tough taskmaster, that one."

As if she'd heard mention of herself, Nurse Tilda marched across the porch with a stern look on her face, her white orthopedic shoes squeaking with each pounding step. She carried a tray of iced tea. Giving Anna and David an appraising look, she said, "Here's your refreshments—compliments of Gladys. I'm Tilda Reynolds, by the way."

Anna and David gave nervous greetings then took their iced teas. David shot Anna a look full of wonder over his glass and was rewarded with a quick grin.

Tilda didn't notice as she turned to the general. "What's all of this?" she asked, clearly concerned for her patient. "Brownies? Isn't it just about dinnertime for you two?"

The general waved a hand in the air. "Ah, now, Tilda, we have guests. We can't be rude to our visitors—they brought the brownies and Trisha baked them. Give us a few minutes, okay? We'll eat our peas and carrots later, we promise."

Tilda pursed her lips and held her plump hands in front of her. "Well, I suppose it won't hurt for Ali to get a little more fresh air or to have a brownie. But it's getting awfully hot out here, sir. Just don't tire him too much."

"We won't stay long," Anna said to reassure the woman. "We just wanted to stop by and say hello."

Tilda shot Anna a hard look then smiled. "You're the woman who runs Children of the Day, right?"

Anna glanced at David. She looked uncomfortable with the description. "Yes, that's me. I'm Anna Terenkov."

"I know your mama," Tilda said, taking a seat on a side chair. "Olga is so much fun. We attend Bible Study together. She has such a sweet spirit. A bit too wild for me, but I like her just the same."

"Really?" Anna smiled. "I'll have to tell Mother I met you. And Tilda, we all appreciate what a great job you're doing, taking care of Ali."

Tilda shook her head and clicked her tongue. "He's so precious. Not a bit of trouble." Then she glared at the general. "But this one, oh, he likes to boss the entire household around."

"It's *my* household," the general replied in his strongest military voice. "You'd be wise to remember that, woman."

Tilda didn't seem the least intimidated, David noted.

"I know my place," the nurse said. "*And* I know my job." Then she stood, clearly not worried about offending the general. "You have fifteen minutes, then I'm coming back out. And I'll have medicine for both of you."

"We will wait with bated breath," the general retorted, waving her away. "Now, be gone and let an old man enjoy a pretty young woman and her soldier friend for a while."

Tilda stomped away, but she winked at David as she walked by him.

"I wouldn't want to get on her bad side," David said, his tone low.

"I stay on her bad side," the general admitted. "But she is good to Ali and she *does* know her job, and that's all that matters to me."

Anna leaned forward. "We brought Ali a present. It's a book of Bible stories." She handed the book to Ali and was rewarded with a beaming smile.

The general looked down at Ali while the little boy looked through the colorful picture book. "We'll read it together at bedtime," he said. "That seems to be one of our favorite times together."

"I'm glad to see you two getting along so well," Anna said, her hand on her heart. "We were so worried."

"Afraid I'd be my usual ornery self?" the general asked, a gleam in his watery eyes. "I guess I've given everyone enough reasons to assume that."

"Well, yes, sir," Anna admitted. "It's just so hard to adjust to something like this. But I think you're both doing a fine job."

"We've had lots of help," General Willis said. "You know our neighbor, Sarah Alpert, I believe."

"We both know her," David said, remembering the pretty redheaded schoolteacher who'd dropped by the Children of the Day offices one afternoon. "She lives next door?" He glanced across the yard to a small yellow cottage.

"Sure does," Marlon said. "And let me tell you, she has sure taken a shine to my grandson. She's been telling him all about what to expect when he starts school here." His expression showed caution. "We have to think positive."

"Sarah loves children," Anna replied.

"I invited her over to get to know him for that very reason and now they're fast friends," Marlon said. "It's good for the boy to have someone younger and more mobile to play out back with him. I'm certainly not as agile as I once was." He coughed long and hard as if to back up that claim.

"Sarah would be delighted, I'm sure," Anna said. "I'm glad she's nearby."

David leaned forward. "Hey, I think I remember Dr. Mike mentioning her a couple of times. They know each other, right?"

Anna nodded. "They…uh…dated a few years back, but things didn't work out."

David didn't want to pry. Mike had never gone into detail about how he knew Sarah and now David understood why. "Well, I'm sure Mike would want Ali to have as many friends as possible, so that's nice that she's nearby."

"And she's easy on the eye," the general said with a smile. "Sarah needs to find a good husband."

Anna laughed at that. "Now, General, you sound like my mother, trying to match up people."

"What about you two?" Marlon asked. "You make a nice couple."

David looked over at Anna, watching as a soft pink blush moved up her neck. "We're just friends," he said to make her more comfortable.

"Yes, just friends," Anna echoed. "David is doing some work at COTD."

"Pity," the general said through a snort as he shook a finger at David. "I just thought—"

"We're friends," David said again. But when he glanced over at Anna, he realized it *was* a pity that they weren't more than that. A real pity.

He just might have to do something to change that.

Chapter Seven

"What do you mean, I did it the wrong way?"

David stared over at Trisha Morrison, thinking the pesky socialite somehow always managed to criticize everything he did. This morning, she'd found him filing away some paperwork and had immediately informed him that he'd put it in the wrong place. She'd somehow managed to single him out from the half dozen other volunteers milling around, which made David wonder if she had it in for him for some reason. When she didn't answer, he leaned forward on the rickety old desk chair. "Well, did I do something horrible to the filing system?"

Trisha looked contrite then shrugged. "I didn't mean to imply you'd done anything wrong, David. I just wanted to help. Anna is meticulous about the filing around here."

She looked so uncomfortable, David almost felt sorry for snapping at her. But the woman made him uneasy, always staring at him. "Anna explained it to me earlier," he said, "but why don't you just show me where these papers go, just in case."

Trisha came around the desk located in the long common room on the other side of the hallway from Anna's office. "Never mind. If Anna told you to do it that way, then it's fine by me." She glanced down at the color-coded files. "I think I looked at the colors and just assumed—"

David lifted an eyebrow, staring her down in much the same way he could stare down a scared soldier. Then he smiled to relieve the anguish he saw in her face. The woman sure was sensitive. "Believe it or not, I know my primary colors. Anna said red for urgent, blue for possible and orange for discussion later. And I have the rest memorized, too. So don't assume, okay?"

They were in the room located just past Caitlyn's desk, where most of the volunteers congregated to stuff envelopes or go through the mail, man the phones and do the daily filing. Today, however, David was alone in what had probably once been part of the parlor, while some of the other volunteers were doing inventory of the kitchen supplies and tidying up the guest rooms. Or he *had* been alone, until Trisha had come sashaying in. Anna had asked him to sort through some of the stacks of paperwork located on an old shelf and to file away whatever needed to be put away, while stacking any urgent papers in a pile on Caitlyn's desk. He'd been doing just that until Trisha had stood over him, waffling between being superior and being scared.

"I said I was sorry," she replied, her brown-eyed gaze darting here and there. "I was only trying to help."

"How would you do this?" David asked, thinking maybe if he enlisted Trisha's help, she'd warm up to him. The girl seemed as jittery as an alley cat caught in a bulldog pen. And just about as flighty as a Texas twister.

Trisha gave him a measured look then shrugged. "Actually, I don't do much filing. Anna says *I* always put things in the wrong place."

David had to grin at that. "So...I'm supposed to listen to your advice anyway?"

She smiled back, her dark eyes lighting up. "Probably not. Just ignore me. It's Monday and I'm in a bad mood."

David took that into consideration. She did have dark circles underneath her eyes. "Long weekend?"

Trisha sank down in a chair, gulping the giant latte she'd brought in with her. "I broke up with my boyfriend—again."

David let out a whistle. "Can't help you there. I'm not very good in the love department."

Her tense expression softened. "I suppose not, since you've been a little occupied on the war front lately. Maybe now that you're back home—"

"Maybe," he said, wondering where Anna had taken herself off to. It seemed the more he flirted with her, the more Anna tried to distance herself from him. "But I think I've lost my touch." And, from the way Trisha was looking at him with such an expectant expression, he wondered if she had noticed his keen interest in her friend. Maybe that was why she seemed so uncomfortable around him. "I guess I just need to stick to business around here anyway."

Trisha's smile was bittersweet. She leaned against the battered oak desk and let out a soft sigh. "Can I ask you a question?"

David nodded, not sure he wanted to hear the question. "Go ahead."

"Do you…do you have feelings for Anna?"

So she *had* noticed. And of course, she wouldn't approve. "Uh, I like her, if that's what you're asking."

"We all *like* her," Trisha said, back to her somewhat snobbish attitude. "What's not to like about Anna? She's hardworking, dedicated, sweet, and she's beautiful." She leaned forward, dropping the pen she'd been twirling. "I need you to promise me something, David."

Surprised by her earnest, direct command, he lifted his chin. "Depends. I'm not so sure I know you well enough to promise much, but go ahead. Hit me with your best shot."

Trisha stared down at her hands. "Anna's my best friend. I need you to promise me that you won't do anything to hurt her."

Puzzled at the intensity of her words, David nodded. "I hadn't planned on hurting anyone. I'm just here to help out while I'm on leave. I can't promise much more than that right now." And while he was attracted to Anna, he wasn't one to rush things and he certainly wasn't going to discuss that with Trisha. "But I do intend to get to know *everyone* around here. Even you."

"Just be careful," Trisha said, the darkness in her eyes showing her sincerity. "Anna guards her heart. She's been that way since I've known her. She lost her father when she was young and now she devotes all of her time to COTD. She rarely dates anyone."

"I get that," David said, somewhat put off by the lecture, especially since it was coming from someone who seemed a bit self-centered. But then, maybe he was misjudging Trisha. "But thanks for the warning. I promise I won't overstep my bounds."

Trisha sat there staring at him for a long time. "You're mad at me now, aren't you?"

David finished stuffing invoices into a folder then got up. "No, not exactly. I just don't get why you feel it's necessary to explain things to me. It's almost as if you think I'm not good enough for Anna."

Trisha began fidgeting with the ink pen again, her eyes downcast. "I never meant it to sound that way. It's complicated."

"Yeah, it must be. 'Cause I don't get it. And I guess I don't get you. Are you jealous of Anna possibly finding happiness of her own?"

"Of course not," she said. Then she got up, her eyes bright, her skin flushed. "But…I do wish you'd give *me* a chance, David."

David scratched his head. "So…you'd rather I flirt with you than Anna?"

"No, oh, no," she said, shock marring her expression. "It's not like that. Not like that at all. You and I…we can't…I mean, that would be silly. I have a boyfriend."

"Sure you do, even if you broke up with him, right?"

"Right. And I'm going to call him right now."

He grinned up at her. "Good idea. Work on your own love life and leave mine alone."

"You're right." Trisha grabbed her purse and rushed toward the front door. "I'm certainly not the best person to issue advice around here."

David got up and thought about making Trisha continue this discussion, but he'd had enough of her superior attitude. Before he could decide, the front door opened and Olga walked in.

"What's wrong?" Olga asked, looking from Trisha's retreating back to David, standing inside the office.

"I have to go," Trisha said over her shoulder, her head down. Then she bolted out the door, her high-heeled mules clip-clopping on the hardwood floor of the porch.

Olga lifted her arched brows in a question aimed at David. "What happened here?"

David sank down in one of the old leather chairs in the lobby. "I have no idea. One minute she was giving me advice about everything from filing papers to being careful in my love life, then the next she was heading for parts unknown. She's a very high-strung girl, isn't she?"

Olga's smile was indulgent, but confused. "Yes, she is. But remember, she's all alone. I think she's just afraid right now. And when we're afraid, we put up a good front. You remind her of things she doesn't want to think about—you being a returning soldier, that is."

David nodded. "I don't think she likes having me around."

Olga came over to face him then leaned back against one of the rickety tables near his chair. "You probably remind her of her father. He was a very strict military man."

"I'm not that way, at least not with most people," David said. "I've tried to be nice to Trisha, but…I get this feeling she either resents me or doesn't think I'm worth the effort."

Olga patted her puffy hair, her shy smile belying the knowing look in her eyes. "We're all worth the effort, David. Maybe Trisha just needs someone to show her that. She's grasping at straws right now, trying to decide how to handle being left with her father's legacy. I think she's taking out her frustrations on you."

"Because I'm a soldier?"

"Possibly. Or maybe because you could come between Trisha and her best friend."

"You mean, Anna?"

Olga nodded, her smile tightening. "I do mean Anna. We've all noticed how you two have been spending time together. While some of us approve, Trisha might resent that."

"Oh, I have no doubt about that," David replied. He got up, suddenly tired of defending himself. "I guess some things never change."

"What do you mean?" Olga asked, her painted nails clutching her gathered denim skirt.

"I mean, maybe it was a mistake for me to come back here," he said. Then he headed for the door.

When Anna returned from her errands, she found Olga sitting in her office. "Hey, Mother. What's going on?"

Olga glanced up from a thick report file. "Oh, hi, honey. I was just going over our proposed budget for next year. Looks as if you have everything in order."

Surprised, since Olga rarely asked about the budget, Anna put her packages in a corner and sat down across from her mother. "Okay, now tell me what's really going on? Where is everyone?"

Olga gave her an eloquent shrug. "Caitlyn is having lunch with Steve and the girls. Trisha rushed out of here like a tumbleweed in a windstorm and David left shortly after that. Something sure is brewing between those two."

Her mother's pointed look made Anna's heart pound with all the intensity of a military drum. Olga could be tenacious when trying to find out things. "Did Trisha say where she was going?"

Olga's eyebrows lifted. "No, she did not."

"And what about David? Did he seem upset?"

Again, the lifting of her mother's eyebrows. Which only meant Olga would pry the truth out of her. "He seemed almost disappointed. Said it had been a mistake, him coming back here."

Anna grabbed her purse again. "I have to find David, Mother. Will you stay by the phones?"

Olga frowned, but nodded. "Of course, dear. But what is going on around here? Anna, is there something you need to tell me?"

"I can't tell you right now," Anna said as she headed for the door. "But soon, Mother."

Olga put a hand to her heart. "I've certainly heard that before."

The phone rang, causing Anna to halt.

Olga grabbed it, putting a hand up to her throat. "Oh, hello, Reverend Fields. Anna—she's just on her way out."

Anna started back in, but Olga motioned for her to go. "I'm glad I caught you, Reverend," Olga said, smiling at Anna. "I wanted to go over my ideas for increasing church attendance. What did you think about the speed-dating possibility?"

Anna cringed then mouthed, "Mother!" Honestly, her mother could be so impetuous at times. Speed-dating at church! That would sure give the charter matrons yet another reason to wag their tongues about her mother's behavior.

Olga's smile was pure serenity. "But, Reverend

Frank, it could be fun, bringing people together to get to know each other. I don't think it would be so bad. We could have a theme that included a particular Bible verse."

Apparently, the good reverend didn't agree with her mother's quirky idea of getting church members together. Olga's smile quickly turned into a frown. "Well, if that's how you feel then I suppose…"

"Mother?" Anna called, "does he need to speak to me?"

"No, Anna," Olga said, her tone exaggerated. "The Reverend said he'd call back. Go on with you, now."

Anna shook her head, feeling sorry for the hapless Reverend Fields. When her mother set her mind on something, it wasn't easy to dissuade her. And Anna had a very distinct feeling that Olga was gunning for the stoic widower. After all of these years, her mother was trying to get back into dating.

"I can't deal with that right now," Anna mumbled as she got into her beat-up old tan Jeep. "I have to find David."

And if she couldn't find him, she needed to find Trisha. Dialing her cell while she waited for the traffic light onto Veterans Boulevard to turn green, Anna was relieved when Trisha answered. "Trisha, are you all right? Mother said David and you had some kind of altercation."

Trisha moaned low. "It wasn't like that. We just rub each other the wrong way. He hates me, Anna."

Anna held her breath, then drove through the intersection, careful to watch the traffic as she talked. "You didn't—?"

"No, I didn't tell him anything," Trisha replied. "Look, I'm at the Coffee Break. Can you take a few minutes to come here?"

"I'm near there now," Anna said. "I'm on my way."

David exited the gate at Fort Bonnell and headed up Veterans Boulevard. Not sure what to do with himself this afternoon, he thought about going back to Children of the Day just to see if Anna was there. But then, he didn't want to run into Trisha again.

Glancing at the restaurants along the green, he noticed Anna's Jeep parked in front of the Coffee Break. David pulled his truck up besides hers, thinking if he could catch her away from the chaos of her office, they might be able to have an uninterrupted conversation. He'd just parked and got out when he saw Anna and Trisha huddled together at a bistro table near the front window of the coffee shop.

And it looked as if Trisha was crying.

Thinking he'd upset her more than he realized, David debated whether to go in and join the women or just keep walking. He wanted to see Anna, but he didn't want to rehash anything with Trisha. He wasn't one to go around making women cry. Not on purpose, at least.

He was just about to turn around and leave when he felt a tug on his arm. "Hey there, Chief Ryland, sir."

David turned to find Maddie Bright smiling up at

him as she went into a formal salute. David saluted back. "Maddie, how are you? And…at ease, soldier." His grin made her relax, but she kept smiling.

"I'm good," the perky nurse said. "Getting adjusted to being back on post. How are you?"

"I'm okay," David said, keeping one eye on the two women in the coffee shop. "I was just…going for something cool to drink. Want to join me?"

Maddie shook her head. "I've got to go to the bank and take care of a few things. Have you seen Ali?"

David told her about the visit he and Anna had had with Ali and the general. "He looks better, but he still tires easily. We didn't stay long."

Maddie nodded. "I'm going to visit him again soon. I miss him."

They chatted a while, then said goodbye. After he watched her walk away, David turned back toward the coffee shop.

And saw Anna and Trisha staring at him through the window. They both looked torn between being friendly or running the other way. He waved, wishing he could have made a fast getaway. But it was too late. Now he'd have to at least go inside and say hello.

He only hoped whatever was bothering Trisha wouldn't put a damper on his friendship with Anna. He didn't want that. Deciding he'd just have to win Trisha over so he could continue getting to know Anna, David smiled then opened the door.

He loved a good challenge.

Chapter Eight

Anna cautioned Trisha. "Be nice. If you keep antagonizing the man, he'll become even more suspicious. And that won't help matters when you do decide to tell him the truth."

Trisha looked away. "I know. I need to pray about my attitude, but honestly this is just so hard to deal with. I'll be polite then leave. I'm sorry, but this is just so awkward."

Anna didn't have time to give any more advice to her friend. David came over to their table, a hesitant smile on his face. "Ladies, how's it going?"

"Good, good," Trisha said, avoiding a direct stare. Then she finally glanced up at him. "David, I'm sorry for my behavior earlier. Chalk it up to the boyfriend thing. I took my frustrations out on you, and I shouldn't have done that." She glanced over at Anna. "We had a good talk and as always, Anna has helped me to see things in a different light. I don't deserve such a good friend."

Anna watched David's expression. He seemed to soften toward Trisha. "That's okay. I understand. I didn't mean to get you all riled up."

Trisha grabbed her huge leather purse. "You didn't. But I'm calling it a day. I'm not any help to anyone today." She got up. "Here, take my seat. You and Anna can go over the merits of our elaborate filing system."

Anna was pleased when David smiled again, so she decided to stick to business. "Trisha told me you were giving a valiant effort with the files. We're trying to go to more of a paperless filing system, but that takes new computers and lots of funding."

He moved aside as Trisha stood. "A good idea, though. In the meantime, I'll try to follow the flow. I just hope I don't put something in the wrong place."

Trisha leaned down to kiss Anna's cheek. "Thanks for the pep talk. I'll call you later." She gave David a reluctant look then left the coffee shop.

"She hates me," David said as he settled into the vacant chair.

"It's not that," Anna replied, wishing with all her heart she could explain. "Trisha seems a bit spoiled, I know, but she has a big heart. She's very devoted to our cause and that makes her a bit territorial, I think."

"And very devoted to shoes and accessories and having her way, too," he retorted. "Which makes her very spoiled in my opinion." Then he looked embarrassed. "I'm sorry. I shouldn't judge her, but she seems to be all over the map, emotionally. Maybe she needs to talk to your mother."

Anna looked away, out the window. When a young waitress showed up to take David's order, she waited before commenting. He ordered coffee, black, with apple pie and ice cream before he settled back to stare at her. At least his appetite was intact. Unlike Trisha's. She was nearly skin and bones from worry and grief.

"Trisha's been to see both my mother and Reverend Fields," she explained, hoping to convey sympathy for her friend. "But you have to understand, she's overwhelmed right now. She's all alone in the world, with no living relatives. And she's inherited not only a great amount of wealth, but the weight of her father's reputation, too. She's afraid she'll fail, on every level."

He raked a hand over his chin. "I guess we all feel that way at times, with money or without. So what's going to happen to her?"

Seeing the sincere concern in his eyes, Anna prayed she'd get through to him. "I don't know. I'm trying to advise her. She's setting up an endowment for Children of the Day, based on her father's wishes, so that's good. And she does work hard for us. Today was just a bad day for her since she had another fight yesterday with Nick. They make up and break up on a weekly basis. She thinks he might be with her only because of her money, but Nick keeps trying to convince her that he loves her. Trisha is really a good person, so she's susceptible to his persuasion. You two need to start over and get to know each other better."

He leaned forward. "I'd like that." He shrugged. "But right now, I'd rather talk about you. This wasn't what I had in mind for our first date."

"I didn't realize this was our first date," she replied, her heart jumping to a rapid beat.

"Well, I'm going to take you out soon. On a real date."

"Confident in that, are you?"

"Yes. I'm a lot more confident now than when I grew up here. But now, well, things seem to be looking up."

Anna could understand that. "I didn't fit in when I came here, either. My accent made me stand out, and when people found out I grew up in Russia, well, it was as if I had a plague or something. Now it's home."

He looked over at her, a new realization seeming to dawn in his eyes. "I guess that would be hard. At least I was born here, even if my father never claimed me." He gave her a challenging look, as if to see whether she'd condemn him, too.

Anna wanted to encourage, not condemn. "Tell me about your childhood some more. You don't talk about your mother very much."

He shrugged. "My childhood was hard. No money and no hope. And a mother who refused to let me in on her secrets."

"So you don't remember anything about your father?"

"All I know about the man is that he left me a trust

that helped my mother pay for things when I was growing up. There's a small bank account left from that money—mine whenever I need it. I don't need it and I certainly don't want it. But she refuses to tell me anything beyond that. I guess it would be even harder though, knowing my dad than losing him the way you and Trisha both lost yours."

She nodded, her hands on her frappacino cup as she tried to weigh her words. "It's not easy, either way. *You* probably wonder about what might have been, and *I* remember what could have been. After my father's death, my mother was determined to bring me to the United States. He had had friends from Texas, and she loved his stories about this state. So this is where we landed. She was very brave to do that. Brave and a bit impulsive, but then, that's my mother."

"You two sure seem different."

"Like night and day," she said, smiling. "But I love her and I admire her spirit. As for me, I've always been more of a wallflower."

"You are not that," David said, his tone full of reproach. "Don't sell yourself short, Anna. It takes all kinds to make the world go round. Even spoiled socialites, I reckon."

Anna grinned, feeling better about things. "So you'll give Trisha a chance?"

His gaze held hers, a look of longing coupled with doubt in his eyes. "For you, yes."

"Don't do it for me," she replied, the heat of his

promise making her feel warm. "Do it for Trisha. She needs friends around her right now."

"Don't we all?"

"Yes, that's why I want to get to know you better, too. I care about you."

His gaze brightened. "Really? You care about me?"

"Of course I do," she said, a gentle heat moving up her neck. "You've done so much for us already, bringing Ali home, helping out at the offices." Just to put a bit of levity back into the situation, she added, "But, all of that aside, I think I'd like that date you promised, but let's keep things professional for a while longer. Just so people don't talk too much. My work has to come first."

He looked sheepish. "I hadn't thought about that. I'll try to behave myself from now on." He leaned close. "I can be very professional when I need to, but with you, Anna, that might be tough."

Anna thought the same thing. The man had a certain charm that just shouted "bad boy." But he also oozed confidence and the kind of masculine strength that inspired women to want to nurture his troubled soul. He was trained as a pilot and a soldier, but she wondered if he wasn't terrified of anything smacking of emotional issues. Maybe that was why he felt so helpless around women at times.

"I do appreciate you, David," she said, pushing away the erratic feelings threatening her own code of professionalism. "And I'd like to keep you as a volunteer."

He took a sip of his coffee. Leaning back in his chair, he said, "I'd like a little more than just appreciation, Anna. And I'd like to be more than just a volunteer."

Anna wasn't sure how to respond to that drawling, husky request. "I can't promise much more than that right now," she said. "That and friendship, of course."

"It's a start," he replied, saluting her with his coffee, while his eyes held hers with hope.

"It *is* a start," Anna said, her words breathless with her own hopes and fears.

Later that day as David sat watching the news in his apartment on post, he thought back over his talk with Anna. She seemed very loyal to her friend Trisha, but then women were known to hold special bonds with each other. Bonds that didn't include clueless men. But he had to wonder if Anna had been warning him away, too. She'd made it sound as if she didn't need anyone in her life. Anyone like him, that is.

"You're not exactly in her life yet, bud," he told himself as scenes from the war front moved across the TV screen. While the scenes brought back powerful memories for David, Anna's soft smile helped him to live in the present moment. "I'm home," he said to the screen. "And, I think I'm done."

He'd thought long and hard about his upcoming retirement. While he didn't regret his years in the army, David felt a kind of yearning for something else now. He had been proud to serve his country, but this restless feeling deep inside just wouldn't go away. And he thought he knew where it was coming from.

Dear Lord, I need to find out who my father is. David didn't even know if his father was still alive. But he did know that now that he was home and back in Prairie Springs, he needed to find out the truth.

Having stated that silent prayer, David closed his eyes and thought back over his childhood. He could still see his mother in her army uniform, coming home from work. She always walked in the door with a kind of tired look on her face. She'd tell the babysitter thanks, then turn to David, her arms out.

"Come give Mama a hug," she'd say, pride making her pretty in spite of her tiredness.

David would run to her, knowing he was safe caught up against that stiff camouflage, the greens and tans of her uniform coloring his whole world. In the early years, he'd never questioned Sandra about his father; he hadn't known to question until he'd gone to school and heard the taunts from the other children.

"My mama says you don't have a daddy, David."

"Why do you live in that old trailer, David? My mama says only trash lives in a place like that."

So he'd come to believe that he was trash, not worth anyone's time or attention. And he'd begun to resent his mother, especially when she refused to tell him the truth.

"But I have a right to know, Mom."

"You don't need to know anything except this," Sandra would say, her smoky voice low and feathery.

"I love you. I have always put you first. And your father loved you. He just couldn't stay here with us, David."

So his father had left a nice chunk of change to ease his conscience. David had found that out one day when the bank statement had been lying open on the kitchen table. And that was the day he and Sandra had gone through a terrible fight and he'd left in a huff, only to wind up over at Lake Austin staring at the hills and the long sunset. All those years, she'd kept so many secrets from him, held him at bay, refusing to answer his questions.

To get back at her, David had enlisted the minute he turned eighteen. Sandra had been so heartbroken after he headed to Fort Rucker for training, she'd left Prairie Springs and moved to Louisiana to be near some relatives. And now, they rarely spoke.

David glanced at the clock. Why had he been punishing his mother for so long? What if he'd died over there without telling her that he understood her sacrifices?

What was holding him back from calling her more often, from trying to make amends?

"The truth, that's what's holding me back," he said to the blaring television.

Then he thought of Anna. She was always so patient, so understanding whenever someone came to her for help. He'd watched her at work over the last two weeks, always amazed at how she could put grieving widows or upset teenagers at ease. And she'd managed to put him at ease, too. Her gentle encouragement regarding her friend Trisha only made David want to be more accommodating and understanding, more forgiving.

He stared at the phone, wanting to call Anna, but knowing he needed to deal with his mother first. How could he enter into a relationship with so much baggage holding him back from true happiness? No wonder he'd never been in a serious commitment with a woman before. He couldn't get past his own feelings of inadequacy.

David turned off the television, then grabbed his Bible, hoping to find some solace in God's word. As he read all about betrayal and secrets, he stumbled upon a verse in Proverbs. *He who follows righteousness and mercy finds life, righteousness and honor.*

David thought about that. He'd been honored as a pilot who helped save lives, but was he an honorable man? How could he be so righteous when he didn't even want to associate with his own mother? He wished he could be close to her again, the way Anna was close to Olga. He thought about Trisha, all alone, without a mother or a father.

"How can I be of help to her, Lord?" he asked, thinking that maybe he could learn compassion and in turn, somehow learn to forgive his own mother her secrets. Would that make him an honorable, righteous man? Or would it just appease his lonely heart?

David closed his eyes and prayed. He let go of all his ill feelings toward Trisha, then he prayed for help in dealing with his mother. While he was praying, the phone rang. Smiling, he looked up toward the ceiling. "Either your timing is perfect, Lord, or somebody is interrupting my prayers." When he picked up the phone, David found the answer.

"Hi, David. It's Trisha Morrison. Can we talk?"

Chapter Nine

"Trisha. Uh, hi."

Not sure what to say next, David took a long breath.

Trisha's hurried words didn't give him time to form the thoughts in his head, however. "Look, David. I'd like to start over with you."

David lifted his gaze Heavenward. "I hear you."

"You do?" Trisha said, the smile in her words coming through loud and clear even though she sounded shaky.

"I do," David replied, unable to tell her that he'd been lifting up his thoughts to God more than to her. But then, God might be sending him a message, too. "So what's the plan?"

He heard a fluttering of papers. "Well, you can start by agreeing to attend the Children of the Day fund-raiser we're planning for Labor Day weekend."

David sat up, alarmed. He remembered a mention

of that, but he had already told Anna he didn't do black-tie events. "How can that help things?"

"You'd be doing me a favor," she said. "Anna needs a date and I think you should take her."

"A date? You want me to ask Anna out on a date to some fancy fund-raiser?"

"Yes. She'll be there in her official capacity, but she won't think about taking someone with her. I mean, I'm planning the seating chart and I just can't bring myself to stick her with some stuffy old colonel or major, know what I mean?"

He had to grin at that. "I think I do. But what if Anna has someone else in mind to take?"

"Trust me, she doesn't," Trisha said, her words rushed. "And she likes you."

"You think so?"

"I do. And I have to admit, I was worried about that, but I've thought it over and I realized I wasn't being fair to either of you. Anna might not date a lot, but she deserves someone special, even if it's for one night."

David sank back on his plaid couch. "And why this sudden change of heart? Didn't you just warn me away from Anna?"

"Oh, that. I was in a bad mood. But I made up with Nick and now I'm feeling better—about a lot of things."

"So now that your love life is back on track, you're trying to fix me up with Anna?"

"I know it sounds silly, but it's not just that. I was just working on this event and well, I thought about how rude I was to you this morning and I wanted to do something special for you. You can come as my guest, but only if you ask Anna to be your date."

David couldn't help but grin. "You have a very strange way of asking for favors, Trisha. Favors with stipulations—is that your usual way of winning friends?"

"Look, I'm trying," she said. She was silent for a minute, then said, "You make Anna smile. And that means a lot to me."

"I'm touched," David retorted. What did he care if he impressed this woman or not? But somehow, he did care. And he'd promised Anna he'd try to get along with Trisha. "Okay, I'll go. But I'll buy my ticket, okay?"

"You don't need to—"

"I insist. That's *my* stipulation."

"You remind me of someone," she said. Then he heard a great gush of breath. "Never mind."

"Probably someone you'd just as soon forget," he replied.

"You're wrong there," she said, her voice going low. "Very wrong. But that's another story altogether."

Before he could ask her what she was talking about, she started talking again. "So, I'll put you down as a yes and you owe me fifty bucks for the ticket. Black tie, by the way. Better get out those dress blues, soldier."

"I haven't worn them in a long time," he said, wishing he could just take Anna on a picnic instead.

"You'll be fine," she retorted. "But you might

want to get your fancy threads to the cleaners for a good press, pronto."

"Okay, Miss Boss, I'll do just that," he said, relaxing now that they'd managed to get through a whole five minutes of bantering back and forth without any tears or regrets. "So, am I on the A-list now?"

He heard her laughter and the relief in her words. "You are, Chief. Just make sure you treat her right or you'll be back on my bad side."

"No, ma'am. Don't want to be there again." Then he brushed a hand over his hair. "Trisha, what made you decide to call me?"

She was quiet for a minute then she said, "I prayed about it. Bye, David. And thanks."

David hung up the phone then sat there staring at it. She'd prayed about it. Maybe Trisha Morrison wasn't so shallow after all. And wasn't it amazing how she'd been praying about him at almost the exact time he'd been praying about her?

"I think I'll call my mother," David said out loud, to confirm his thoughts. Since he was on a roll, he didn't want to stop now.

And after that, he'd figure out a way to ask Anna to attend the benefit with him. That part would be easy, at least.

"Mother, what are you doing?"

Anna stepped into the small corner office where Olga kept all the files on the members of her grief-counseling group. The little office was cramped, but

Olga had put her distinctive touches on it by decorating it with some of the Russian art she'd collected over the years. Two Murano glass goblets and an exquisite Lithuanian crystal bowl sat next to a reproduction of a Fabergé egg on the tiny shelf behind Olga's desk, while several decorative lacquered boxes and some nesting dolls were stacked on the side table near an old brocade chair. The Russian keepsakes should have looked out of place amongst the standard Longhorn and Lone Star mugs and pencil holders, but somehow her mother made it all work.

Olga looked up from the papers scattered all over her desk, her turquoise earrings shimmying as she beamed a smile at Anna. "Oh, hello, darling. I'm going over these compatibility profiles."

"Compatibility profiles?" Anna was almost afraid to ask. "Why?"

Olga clapped her hands together. She wore a different ring on each finger. The multicolored jewels varied in size and shape but the rings were so much a part of her mother's style that Anna didn't even notice the garnets and tiger's eyes winking at her.

"I'm trying to match up single church members who have things in common," Olga said, her green eyes sparkling. "Isn't it exciting, Anna-bug? Oh, I'll have to remember to get David to fill in a profile."

Anna let out a low moan. "Mother, really, why do you insist on doing such things?"

Olga dropped one of the index cards she had scattered all around her. "What do you mean?"

Anna plopped down into a chair across from Olga then threw her aged canvas-and-leather tote bag down as she crossed one sandaled foot over her khaki-clad knee. "You know—this constant need to meddle in other people's lives?"

"Is that what you think I'm doing?" Olga asked.

"Well, yes. Everyone thinks that's what you're doing."

Olga stopped smiling, her hand clutching her throat. "I don't see a thing wrong with trying to help people find each other, Anna. I mean, we all get lonely now and then. Don't you?"

Anna knew better than to answer that pointed question. Olga's fervent prayer was that Anna would find a good man and settle down to give her grandchildren. Lots of them.

Olga sat quietly waiting, of course. Only a mother could stop all chatter to stare at a child like that.

"I stay too busy to get lonely," Anna said, trying to believe it. But she saw something there in her mother's pretty eyes that made her stop and think, and ask her own question. "What about you, Mother? Are you lonely?"

Olga went back to being her coy self. "Me? Oh, honey, you know I have a full and active life."

"Sure you do," Anna replied, not quite convinced. "And just how *are* things going around here?"

Olga got up to come around the desk, her always-busy hands fluttering as she picked the morning paper off the side table. "Well, we still haven't heard a word from Whitney and John and we're all beside ourselves. I hope those kids are okay. It's all over the news wires, so maybe someone will see or hear something over there."

Anna had been referring to her mother's ongoing flirtation with Reverend Frank, but now she pushed that thought aside to concentrate on something that needed her prayers. "I'll try calling around again. We thought we had some concrete information the other day. Someone thought they recognized them being held inside an insurgent compound. But that source didn't pan out."

Olga threw down the paper and started wringing her hands. "We both know what can happen during a war, Anna. We both sure know that. Soldiers go missing. Some never come home. Sometimes there are just no answers."

Feeling bad for chastising her mother earlier, Anna got up and hugged Olga close. "Yes, we sure do. We'll keep praying for them, Mommy."

Olga stood back then put a hand on Anna's cheek. "You called me Mommy. You haven't called me that in a very long time."

Anna stared at her mother, searching for some sort of crack in that brilliant Olga armor. "No, I haven't, have I? You know, you and I should take off and go to lunch. We haven't had a good long lunch together in a while."

Olga clapped her hands again. "What a perfect idea. And just what I need today. I think that adorable little boutique over on Spring Street is having a clearance sale. And I saw a dress there recently that would look fabulous on you, darling."

Anna couldn't stop the laughter bubbling over as they grabbed their purses to head out the door. "I do need a new dress for the COTD benefit."

Olga touched a hand to her arm. "I suppose I'd better look for one myself." She leaned close, her smile full of a covert mischief. "I'm very compatible with Reverend Fields. Isn't that marvelous?"

Anna was about to answer that when they looked up to find the good reverend himself standing in the middle of the hallway like a deer caught in headlights, his eyes wild with fear, his hair standing up in gray-tinged tufts of brown.

Anna blushed her embarrassment while Olga preened and smiled. "Oh, hello, Reverend."

Reverend Franklin Fields gave them a stony look that reminded Anna of just how quiet and standoffish the man could be. He wasn't very outgoing, but his quiet strength more than made up for his lack of personality. Handsome in a brooding sort of way, the reverend was more than willing to console his church members, though he didn't talk much about himself. But Anna figured her mother probably never let the man get a word in, anyway.

"Ladies."

He made to leave, but Olga shot out in front of him. "I don't know if you heard what I was telling Anna, but I have some interesting news."

He just stood there, a patient smile on his face. "And what is your news, Mrs. Terenkov?"

Olga rushed on. "I did our profiles and surprise, surprise, you and I have a lot in common."

That revelation didn't seem to go over too well with him. "What are you talking about?"

Olga looked practically girlish. "Oh, you remember. We talked about my singles group and ideas to bring people together. I gave you a profile sheet to fill in, remember?"

"I'm sorry, but I threw that in the trash," he replied, giving Anna a look that clearly said "Help me."

"I know you did," Olga said. "But I filled one out for you, based on what little I know about you, of course."

"Mother!" Anna couldn't believe the lengths Olga would go to. And since when was her mother so needy for a man's attention? "That wasn't very tactful."

Olga didn't bat an eye. "I know a lot about this man, darling," she said, smiling at the confounded minister. He frowned and glanced around while Olga recited the facts. "I know he loves faith music and that he likes to read a lot. He likes old movies, especially *film noir*. And I do believe—"

"Stop right there, Mrs. Terenkov," Reverend Fields said, holding up a hand. "You obviously know more about me than I give you credit for, which might show you we're not really compatible at all. I'm a rather boring person."

"So you don't agree that we seem compatible?"

The minister shook his head, a wry smile on his flushed face. "But I do agree that we're friends and that you are a valuable volunteer around here. Now, if you'll excuse me—"

He turned and hurried toward his office, then quickly slammed the door shut.

"Did you hear him?" Olga said, unfazed by his obvious rebuke. "He said we're friends."

"Mother, I don't think he's interested," Anna said, feeling sorry for both of them.

"Oh, but he is," Olga insisted. "He just doesn't know it yet."

Anna didn't argue with her mother. What was the point? She hated to see Olga get hurt, and she wasn't sure how to handle this side of her mother. Olga had never even looked at another man since her father's death. Why now?

"Mother, what's really going on with you, anyway? You've always been out there, but this brings things to a new height. Are you sure you're okay?"

"Oh, it's going to be all right. You'll see," Olga said, lifting her gaze upward in aggravation. "Stop being such a stick-in-the-mud, honey. Besides, I want to talk about you and David. How's that going?"

In spite of her upbeat tone, Anna noticed her mother's shaky voice and saw the darkness coloring her eyes. Maybe Olga wasn't so confident after all. Maybe she was just as lonely and afraid as Anna.

Chapter Ten

"Is that the last of it?"

David sent a hopeful look to Laura Dean. The cute blonde was Anna's secretary, but she was also a dynamo who did a little bit of everything around the COTD offices. And this morning, she'd had David hopping with all her orders and requests to get over one hundred care boxes taped up and ready to take to the shipping company.

"I do believe that's it, sir," Laura said, grinning over at David. "You sure worked up a sweat."

"I'm old and I think I've got early arthritis," David said as he reached for his water bottle. "That was some kind of job, packing all those boxes."

Laura nodded as she checked off things on her list. "Tell me about it. We do it at least once a month."

"And take care of all the other things around here, too," David said, impressed. When he heard voices in one of the rooms down the hall, he glanced at Laura. "What kind of meeting are they having back there?"

Laura put down her clipboard. "Youth counseling for teenagers who have a parent in the war, or worse, have lost a parent in the war. Sometimes both parents. It's hard for them, but the surviving spouse or family doesn't always know how to handle a teenager's grief. So we offer them a quiet place just to vent."

David wiped his brow, thinking about the young twins Caitlyn was now raising for that very reason. "Wow, I guess I haven't thought much about that. Wish I'd had someone to talk to when I was young."

Laura smiled over at him. "We counsel adults, too, sir."

Surprised, David shrugged. "I'm doing okay, thanks. I talk to Chaplain Steve a lot and I'm trying to find the courage to get to know Anna's mother a little better."

Laura giggled at that. "Miss Olga is awesome. I mean, after all they've been through, she and Anna are such an inspiration to all of us."

David had witnessed Laura's loyalty to her employer as evident in how hard she worked to make sure Anna's days ran like clockwork. "You try to shield Anna from a lot, don't you?"

"That's my job," Laura said, bobbing her head. "Anna gave me a chance when I was in a bad way and for that, I'll always be grateful. Working here doesn't pay as much as I could make out in the regular world, but I don't care. I intend to work in nonprofit for the rest of my life and hope that after I finish college I can keep working with COTD in a different capacity."

David let out a whistle then shook his head. "When did young people get so smart? Wish I'd had my life figured out when I was your age."

Laura frowned. "But you did, didn't you? You've made a career out of the army, right?"

David shook his head again. "No, more like the army made a career out of me. But I don't regret the time I've served."

Laura looked up as she heard footfalls creaking just outside the open door, causing David to turn and find Anna standing there smiling at them.

"Spoken like a true soldier," Anna said by way of a greeting. Then she inspected all the neatly stacked mailing boxes lined up against the walls of the supply room. "I see Laura roped you into doing the heavy lifting."

David lifted an arm to show off his biceps. "I don't mind, Chief. I've got plenty of muscle."

Anna and Laura both laughed, causing David to give them a mock frown. "I do have muscle, don't I?"

Even though Anna looked impressed, Laura leaned close to her boss. "He was just complaining about arthritis earlier."

Anna pursed her lips. "Maybe he was trying to get out of some of his duties?"

David put his hands on his hips. "I am not one to shirk my duties, ladies."

"Okay, we believe you," Anna said. "So don't let me stop you." Then she heard a door slamming down the hall. "But I can find you some relief. We've got teenagers in the house today. I'll go round up a couple of them to help you load the van."

"Thanks, I think," David said.

Anna gave him that beautiful smile that seemed to linger. "Just remember, they can smell fear a mile away. Don't show any sign of weakness."

David felt weak at the knees right then. "I'll keep that in mind," he said. "It's been a while since I've been around young people."

She crossed her arms then leaned back against the doorjamb. "You're not that old yourself, Chief."

"Getting there though, *Chief*," he retorted with a grimace. "But I'd at least like to have a family of my own before I croak so I *can* experience being around children and young people again. But it has to be right. I don't want any kid of mine feeling neglected or abandoned."

Anna looked up, a confused expression on her face. "You have plenty of time for that, I think. And I can't imagine you ever neglecting your family."

David couldn't help but ask. "What about you? Do you ever think about having a family?"

She waved a hand toward the boxes. "One day. But this is my family right now."

End of subject, David thought as he watched her whirl and hurry back up the hallway to her office. He looked at Laura. "Sorry I asked."

Laura gave him an understanding smile. "She doesn't like to talk much about her personal life."

"I'll have to remember that," David replied.

Anna was sorry she'd brought up the subject of family with David. It only reminded her that she knew all about his father, but he didn't. What a predicament.

I don't like this, Lord. I don't like withholding something so important from him. What should I do?

Her head down, Anna clutched the ornate silver cross at her throat, her mind racing with a stream of steady prayers.

"Where'd you get the cross necklace?"

She looked up to find David standing at the front door. Before she could respond, he added, "I was about to head out back to pull the van around to take the packages to the shipping company. Want to ride along?"

Anna sat back in her chair, hesitant to talk to him. "Which question do you want me to answer first?"

He seemed to take that as an invitation to come into her office. "May I sit?"

"Of course. You probably need a rest, and the boys aren't quite through with the counseling session anyway. So as Max at the café would say, 'Take a load off.'"

He settled into the chair across from her with a big grin. "You're cute when you use American slang, you know?"

"Really?"

"Really. You have that little bit of a Russian accent and it…it really gets me."

"It *gets* you?"

He leaned forward, his smile smooth and enticing. "I like it," he said. "A lot."

Anna was sure she felt a case of the nervous hives coming on. "Wasn't I suppose to answer some questions?"

"About my questions," he said, his hands clashed in front of him. "I'm sorry if I seem intrusive, but Anna, I need to know—"

"My father gave me this necklace before he went to Afghanistan," she said, hoping to stall anything more intimate between them. But she had seen that need for closeness in his eyes. "And I have work to do, so I can't go with you to ship the boxes."

He nodded, let out a breath. "Here's the thing, Chief. I've known you for two whole weeks now and during that time, I've thought about asking you out to dinner or something—that first-date thing. In fact, I'd like to escort you to that fancy fund-raiser Trisha's all worked up about. But I'm afraid to ask you. I can't read you, Anna. That's my main question. Is there something about me that concerns you? Are you afraid of me?"

He wanted to take her to the COTD fund-raiser? Anna's heart lifted at the thought of it. David in his dress blues, escorting her into the dinner? She could certainly go for that.

But what would Trisha say?

Anna placed her hands on her desk pad, careful to form the right words. "David, you've been such a help to us—"

"Forget all my good deeds," he interrupted. "I'm not trying to win points with you. I enjoy helping and besides, we've already had the volunteer/friend conversation. So what's the deal, Anna? Just level with me."

"There is no deal," she said, wishing she could tell him the truth. "My concern is that because you *are* one of my volunteers, I'd hate to ruin a good thing."

"You mean, by dating me?"

"It could get uncomfortable, yes. And as you said, we've already had this conversation."

His direct look burned away all her qualms. "I won't always be a volunteer. I only have a few more weeks of R & R and I'll be going to visit my mother for some of that time. Then I'll get right back to work. So I won't be here nearly as much come fall. We'd barely get to see each other, except when I call you to ask you out, of course."

She hid her smile behind what she hoped was a professional demeanor. "Then maybe it's a good idea for us to hold off on anything until then."

"*Anything* like you and me getting together, you mean?"

"Yes," she said, hoping he'd understand. "It's just that we're so busy now with getting ready for the fundraiser and the normal daily operations around here."

"I get it," he said. "So you won't even consider letting me take you to this shindig?"

She thought about that again. The fund-raiser was two weeks away. Maybe Trisha would have told him by then, which would mean that he wouldn't want to take her anywhere. Or maybe he'd forgive her her part in this secret. Either way, Anna couldn't commit to anything until Trisha decided what to do. "Can I think about it?"

He didn't look happy. He sat up then leaned over the desk. "Think all you want to, Anna. But I'm willing to get into my dress blues and a tie just to see you in a ball gown. So…even if I can't take you to this hot-ticket affair as my date, I'll be there waiting for you and I'll surely find you and ask you to dance. Think about that while you're trying to convince yourself to stay away from me, okay?"

With that, he got up, tipped his hand in a salute and left her sitting there, her mind reeling. Anna put her head in her hands and groaned. How much longer could she pretend? How much longer could she deny she had feelings for David Ryland? And how much longer could she carry this burden of knowing that the truth would probably destroy him? And their relationship.

David took out his frustrations on the boxes he had to get loaded within the next hour. With a grunt and a quick lift, he managed to send one of the boxes to the front of the big van's cargo compartment as he mumbled to himself.

"I don't get women."

"That makes two of us."

David turned to find a scrawny teenaged boy with shaggy brown hair staring up at him. "Hello," he said, reaching out a hand to the boy. "I'm David."

The kid took his hand and shook it with surprising strength. "I'm Brandon. Brandon Matthews. I'm supposed to be helping you."

"Well, don't look so excited about it," David retorted, his surliness matching the teen's.

"I'm not," Brandon shot back. "Jeff was supposed to help, too, but he bolted."

David looked around at the quiet backyard. "So it's just you and me, huh?"

Brandon shrugged then grabbed a box. "I reckon."

"How old are you?" David asked as he picked up the next box.

Brandon hopped up into the van. "Just hand 'em to me," he ordered. Then he said, "I'm sixteen."

David remembered sixteen. Tough age. Memories of his mother sitting alone at the old dining table, paying bills hit him square in the gut. Which caused David to send yet another box of supplies toward the front of the van with enough force to rattle the old vehicle.

"Hey, man, you trying to break all the cookies we packed?"

David looked up at Brandon. "Sorry. I guess I'm used to heavier supplies."

"Yeah, well, lighten up. One of these boxes could be headed to where my dad is."

David mentally slapped himself. Of course Brandon would have someone over on the front. He'd been in the session. "Is he in the Middle East?"

Brandon nodded then spouted off the name of his dad's battalion. "He's special ops."

David knew what that meant. The kid's father probably rarely got to contact him, let alone tell his son where he was or what he was doing. And he probably wouldn't get any of these cookies. "That's the best of the best," he said, hoping to console the kid.

"Or the worst of the worst," Brandon shot back, his surliness intact. "It's dangerous."

David tried again. "How are things at home?"

"You some kind of counselor, too?"

"No, just curious." David hefted another box. "I grew up without a dad. It's hard sometimes."

Brandon didn't respond. Instead, he just kept loading boxes. David granted him the silence he seemed to demand until they were finished. "Want to go with me to ship these out?"

Brandon gave him a "whatever" grunt, but he hopped in the van.

"Do you need to call home and let them know?"

"My mom's at work. She can't be bothered."

David also remembered those days. "So you're back in school?"

"Not yet."

Which meant the kid pretty much did whatever he wanted without supervision. Anna had warned him that a lot of the youths who stopped by COTD felt ignored and neglected. So that meant they'd get bored and take any opportunity to get into trouble or skip school during the year.

But she hadn't warned him about how much seeing one of them up close and personal would bring back all his own angst and anger, and make him remember how he'd managed to do the same thing.

"How about a hamburger and milkshake at the café after we're finished? My treat."

"Whatever."

David shifted the creaking gears of the old van and headed out toward the shipping office, wondering how he could help this kid.

I need You, Lord, he thought. *I need You not only to help this angry kid, but to help me with my own anger, too.*

And, he thought with a wry smile, *I need You to stop sending me so many signs. I get the message, Lord. Loud and clear.*

Maybe this was exactly why Anna was being so standoffish. Maybe this bitterness and anger was the *something about him* that she just couldn't deal with.

Chapter Eleven

"You and Brandon seem to be getting along."

Anna was glad to see David walking into the kitchen so bright and early on a Saturday morning, but the scowl on his face made her wish she'd just kept her mouth shut about Brandon. But he and the teen had been spending a lot of time together so she couldn't help but be curious. It seemed to her they'd both benefit from the company.

"The kid needs somebody and I have plenty of time on my hands right now," David said, without looking up. He grabbed a cup and poured some of the coffee Anna had just brewed. "He's supposed to meet me here so we can clean out the garage out back. If I build some shelves in there, it would be good for extra storage."

Surprised and pleased, Anna gasped. "I've been trying to get someone to take that job for a very long time. Wow, how'd you get Brandon to agree to help you?"

David shrugged then stared down into his coffee. "It wasn't easy. At first, he copped an attitude a mile wide. But I just stayed with it, I guess. I'm not a trained counselor, but it's not hard to figure out the kid needs some adult male guidance. He's worried about his mom being here all alone and about his dad over there doing such a dangerous job, only he doesn't like to show that."

Anna leaned against the counter to stare out the window. "A lot of these kids are that way. They don't want us to see them upset so they try to be so tough." She wondered if that was how it had been for David growing up, but she didn't dare broach that particular subject.

When he didn't offer up any more explanations or observations, she said, "Anyway, thanks for cleaning the garage. As I said, I've had that on my list for months now."

"I know. Trisha told me."

Surprised that David and Trisha had even communicated over the last week, Anna smiled. She'd tried so hard to concentrate on work the last few days she'd obviously missed out on some of the things happening right in front of her. "You're getting to know a lot of people around here."

"I'm trying."

She didn't miss the hint of cynicism in his statement. Hoping to get him out of his bad mood, she said, "Well, I for one appreciate everything you've accomplished here. The playground seems to be coming along." Anna couldn't believe how much David had done since he'd walked through the doors three weeks ago. And now here he was on a Saturday morning. "You never stop though, do you?"

"Neither do you," he said, finally meeting her gaze. "And since you've managed to avoid me all week long, I think you're finding extra things to keep you occupied."

Anna couldn't deny it. She had been avoiding him. "I'm sorry." Shielding herself with anger, she turned to leave the room. "But you might recall that I founded this place and it's up to me to keep it going. And this week I've been busy helping to set up a video-phone station so people could come in and actually see their loved ones while they talk to them. So if I seem rude, David, I do apologize."

He stopped her before she'd made it to the big arch in the kitchen doorway. "Hey, I'm the one who should be sorry. What you do around here is amazing—temporarily taking in helpless children, putting together all the care packages, helping relatives track down their loved ones—I mean, the list goes on and on and here I am complaining because I haven't seen much of you this week."

Anna let out a long sigh. "That's how it works around here. Even after my day is over, there is always something else to be done. I wake up in the middle of the night, thinking about everything and still I can't seem to accomplish nearly what I'd like to. Sometimes I wonder if it's all worth it."

He pulled her around to face him. "It's always worth it, Anna. Those men and women over there, they need everything you can offer them and then some, and so do their families. The pressure they're under is ugly and dirty and scary and nonstop. And even now that I've been on post for a few weeks, I still have nightmares about it." He ran a hand over his thick hair. "I wake up in a cold sweat, thinking I'm back in my chopper flying over enemy territory to get a litter of injured soldiers off the battlefield. I see the gunners watching for an attack as I try to land my bird. I mean, I have to sit up in bed and remind myself that I'm home now."

Anna saw the horror in his eyes. "Which is why you could probably use someone to talk to now and then, too. I should at least take the time to listen." No matter how miserable she'd be in the process. Even now, she wanted to hug him close and tell him it would be all right, but thoughts of Trisha and the secret they both knew held her back.

He stepped around, frowning. "I don't want you to feel sorry for me. I just want you to— Never mind. I don't know what I want."

"That makes two of us." She leaned against the doorjamb, enjoying the quiet of an early weekend morning even if having David nearby disrupted that quiet. The staff had Saturdays off, but she had volunteers who came in for a few hours on the weekend so she could have a little rest herself, something Olga had demanded years ago after Anna had worked herself into pneumonia one long winter. Needing to make David smile again, she said, "So what are you really doing here today, besides frowning at me?"

He finally did smile, but it was a weak effort. "Don't worry, no hidden agenda such as trying to find some alone-time with the boss. I told you—Brandon and I are going to clean out the storage—"

The front door banged open then slammed back on its hinges. Anna and David turned in shock to find Brandon standing there, tears streaming down his face.

"Brandon?" David hurried toward the boy, catching him as he collapsed against one of the chairs scattered around the entryway. "Brandon, son, what's wrong?"

Brandon wiped at his nose then just sat staring. Anna ran into the kitchen and got a glass of water to bring to him, but when she offered it, Brandon hit at it and the glass went flying.

"Brandon!" David checked to make sure Anna hadn't been hit.

"I'm okay," she whispered, more concerned for the distraught teen than for the wet floor or the broken glass. "Brandon, what's wrong?"

Brandon finally tried to speak but his voice was so hoarse, Anna had to strain to listen. "My dad…is dead."

"Oh, no." Anna sank down on the floor beside Brandon's chair, tears forming in her eyes. "Oh, Brandon. When—"

"They just came to our house a couple of hours ago. Chaplain Steve was with 'em." He shrugged, going still in the chair. "The sun was coming up and

I was up eating some breakfast—I didn't want to be late. I really didn't want to be late."

David glanced over at Anna then back at the boy, his frown now changed to a concerned expression. "Brandon, I'm so sorry. How's your mom?"

"Some people came to sit with her. I think Miss Olga is there."

Anna had heard her mother leaving earlier but hadn't opened her bedroom door to find out where Olga was going. But then, Olga didn't like to share such news unless she had to. Her mother always went directly to the family first then she worried about telling everyone else later.

"Does your mother know you left the house?" Anna asked, worried about both Brandon and his mom. "She'll be concerned."

Brandon lifted his chin. "She was calling after me when I ran out the door." When Anna started up, he grabbed her arm. "Don't call her yet, please, Anna. I just…I had to get away."

David nodded to Anna that it would be all right. Then he put a finger to his lips, his gaze moving over the boy's pale face. "Let's just sit here a while, okay?"

Brandon looked straight ahead. Anna's gaze held David's, but she nodded okay. And so they sat as the clock on Anna's desk ticked away the seconds in a slow, calculated cadence. And while they sat, Anna could see Brandon's pain reflected in David's dark eyes. She knew how he felt; each time was like reliving it all over again. The sound of tears and sobs, the heartbreak of seeing your mother crumbling into a ball on the floor, the silence, the awful, endless silence of a scream held tightly inside your soul. How did one bear such heartache? How had her mother?

Anna's heart broke all over again and she realized *this,* more than keeping a secret for her friend, was why she'd held David at bay. She couldn't live with that kind of pain.

She looked over at David, tears forming again in her eyes. He attempted a smile, probably to reassure her. But it didn't work. She watched as he lowered his head and began to pray in a soft whisper. Anna looked at Brandon. The boy sat rigid and unyielding, but David held on to his arm and kept on praying.

Anna closed her eyes and did the same, the quiet of the August morning soothing and palpable as she prayed for Brandon's family and for all the soldiers in harm's way. In the silence, she could hear Brandon's sharp intake of breath, she could hear David's whispers for mercy and love, for grace and strength. Somewhere outside, she heard a hawk's lonely keening call up over the trees. Her gaze moved toward the big windows in Caitlyn's office. Like a touch from God, a piercing shard of pure morning sunlight shot through the windows and made a bright swirling pattern on the hallway rug. Anna stared at it for so long, the light hurt her eyes.

When she looked back up, David was watching her, his eyes devoid of any resentment or bitterness even though he had to be feeling those things for

Brandon's sake. David had known exactly what to do for this troubled young man. He'd understood the silence of unanswered prayers. And the echoes of those prayers that could be answered.

Anna's gaze locked with David's then and she realized something she had suspected since the day David had walked off that plane with Ali.

She was in love with him. She had felt this tugging all along, but today, as he sat silent and steady by a scared young boy and simply held on to that boy with all his might, Anna knew that she loved David Ryland with all her heart. But she wasn't sure what to do about that.

So she, too, held on to Brandon, hoping that connection would keep them both safe by David's side until she could figure out how to deal with this joyous yet painful feeling inside her heart.

Later that afternoon, David stood outside on the tiny back porch of his apartment, his mind reeling as he relived seeing Brandon coming through the door. He had to close his eyes to the great weight of the pain inside his chest.

But you've seen death before, he reminded himself as he felt the heat and humidity of the late-August day hitting him square in the face like a wet handkerchief. He'd lived on the battlefield, taking victims away, some clinging to life, some already gone. He would always hear the sound of roaring engines and whirling rotor blades in his head, inside his dreams.

He'd smell the black scents of fuel oil and hydraulic fluid mixed with the salty smell of sweat dripping from his bulletproof helmet and the metallic smells of sickness and death that always permeated the desert air.

Being a medevac pilot had dominated his life since he'd signed up for the army and trained to be a helicopter pilot at Fort Rucker, Alabama, close to eighteen years ago. And his memories of flying helicopters would be in his blood for a very long time, so why was this particular situation getting to him?

Because it's Brandon. The boy's hurts had grabbed David from the first time they'd met. And though they'd only know each other a short while, Brandon had reminded David so much of himself that being around the boy had brought back all the memories he'd tried to put aside. But it had also brought out all of his protective instincts, too. It was Brandon, it was Anna and the shock and sadness he'd seen on her face and it was the fact that he needed to mourn a father he would never even know. His father had been dead to David for a long time now.

"I don't even know *if* you're alive or dead, but I have to let you go," he said, his hands on his hips as he wondered what to do with himself on this lonely Saturday night. He had to get out of this apartment. And he was trying very hard to keep from calling Anna.

He'd left her with her mother at Brandon's house. David and Anna had taken the boy home and sat with the family for a while, but after telling Brandon he'd be back later, David had bolted. Maybe he was having one of those post-traumatic episodes Chaplain Steve had warned him about. He felt as if his little apartment was closing in on him. He couldn't breathe.

Wanting, needing some sort of connection to life, David got in his truck and left the post to head into Prairie Springs. Somehow, his truck stopped in front of General Willis's house and before he knew it, he was ringing the doorbell.

The friendly housekeeper opened the door. "Well, hello, there. The general didn't tell me you were coming by."

"Uh, he doesn't know," David replied. "I thought I'd check in on Ali."

"Seems to be that kind of night," the woman said, waving him on in. "That is one blessed little boy."

Wondering what the woman was talking about, David went into the large paneled den past the winding staircase. When he heard Ali's laughter, followed by feminine voices, he stopped inside the door, surprised to find Sarah Alpert, Anna and Trisha sitting on the floor playing a board game with Ali. He hadn't seen any of their cars outside.

"David," the general said from his leather recliner. "Come on in and join the party. You know Sarah, don't you?"

David nodded toward the pretty redhead. "Yes. Good to see you again."

Sarah clapped her hands as Ali tugged on her shirt

and pointed to the game. "Nice to see you, too, David. We're having a regular party here."

The general chuckled. "Ali and I were geared up for another lonely bachelor night of popcorn and cartoons. Now I have three lovely women visiting. And one lonely-faced warrant officer. Things are looking up around here."

David looked at Anna and saw the wonder on her face. But he thought he saw something else there, too. Something close to relief, maybe? Trisha on the other hand looked as uncomfortable as always. But she had the good manners to hide that discomfort behind a greeting.

"Hello, David."

"What's going on?" he said, an animated smile on his face for Ali's sake. "Y'all started the game without me?"

"Didn't know you were coming," Trisha said underneath her breath, her gaze moving from David to Anna. Then she added, "We have some pizza left."

David followed her pointing finger to the oak table in one corner where two pizza boxes sat. "Pepperoni?"

"And veggie," the general said, making a face. "For the ladies."

"I might have a slice of whatever's left," David said. "That is, if I'm not interrupting."

"Not at all," the general replied, pointing to Anna and Trisha. "These two were kind enough to walk over from Anna's house and help Sarah entertain Ali while I took care of some business earlier. Now Ali won't let them leave until he beats them at Chutes and Ladders."

David sank down on the floor, acutely aware that Anna had yet to speak to him. "Tough game. But one I used to be pretty good at myself. Mind if I join in?"

Trisha looked up at him, her smile tentative. "I don't mind. Do you, Anna?"

Did he sense a bit of a challenge in that question?

Anna looked as skittish as a cornered filly. "I don't mind at all." Finally, she glanced up at David. "Why don't you take my spot and I'll go and find you something to drink."

"Okay." David watched as she walked away, admiring her worn jeans and long cotton tunic top. Then he leaned close to Trisha. "Is she all right?"

Trisha smiled, watching as Sarah tickled Ali and chattered with him. Then she said, "We're all still a bit rattled by Brandon's dad being killed. I guess everyone just needed to see Ali tonight."

The general leaned forward, letting out a cough. "Tough hearing that news. It never gets easy." The old man stared down at his grandson, his hands folded in his lap. "Ali sure makes it easier on me these days, however. Now, if we can just both stay well." He glanced around as if he expected Nurse Tilda to rush in with more medicine. But it was just Anna, bringing David his drink and a slice of pizza.

David smiled up at her, relief mixed with remorse. "Same here. I had to see him with my own eyes, to make sure he was okay." He high-fived the little boy, causing Ali to giggle.

Trisha nodded her understanding then raked a hand over Ali's dark hair. "This little boy represents hope to us, I think. After all, we all worked on getting him here. He's safe now, but…when something like this happens, we just need some reinforcement I think. We need to know we can make a difference, somehow."

David nodded, thinking maybe Trisha went deeper than he'd given her credit for. Reminding himself that she'd just lost her father, too, he said, "I think you're right. So…it's okay that I came by?"

"Better than okay, David," she said. "Anna needs you here. And it's good to see you again. I mean that."

David didn't know why it felt so good to have Trisha's approval, but her words meant a lot to him. Now, if he could make sure Anna felt the same, he just might make it through this long, hot night and wake up tomorrow with some of that hope Trisha had mentioned.

Chapter Twelve

"So do you want to get a bite to eat?"

David hoped Anna would agree to the quick meal since she'd been burning daylight all day long. They'd just left Brandon's house after having attended a memorial service at church. After sitting with Mrs. Matthews and the rest of the family for a couple of hours, he could tell Anna felt as drained as he did.

Instead of answering his question, she turned in the truck and stared back up at the tiny cottage where Brandon and his mother lived. "Don't you find it strange to hold a memorial when the body hasn't arrived home yet?"

David wasn't sure how to answer that question. He knew a thing or two about dealing with grief, however. "I think the service was to comfort his family more than anything. We need to honor the dead in order to bind together with the living, I reckon."

Anna clutched the tissue in her hand. "We've both

seen too much death, David. Way too much. Sometimes it's just so hard—" She stopped, looked down at her hands. "It's just so hard."

David understood what she was trying to say. Between the oppressive Texas heat and the weight of his grief, his chest tightened with each breath as if he might suffocate. He cranked the truck and took off toward Interstate 10. This time he didn't ask Anna where she wanted to go. He just drove until they were near the river.

"Where are we going?" Anna asked as if she'd just now realized they weren't back at her house.

"To a spot that will bring us some relief," David replied.

"But I have—"

"Whatever it is, it can wait," he interrupted. "Or someone else will be glad to handle it."

For the first time since he'd met her, Anna looked meek and quiet. She lowered her head, her gaze on her hands again. As much as he knew she needed a break, David couldn't handle the look of defeat in her eyes. So he reached across the seat and took one of her hands in his. "It's going to be all right, Anna. I promise."

"No one can make that promise," she reminded him, her eyes misty. "Brandon's father will never come home, except in a body bag. It's not all right. Sometimes, David, I just don't know where to turn."

He squeezed her hand. "You turn to me. You turn to your mother. And you always have the Lord. I've sure leaned on Him a lot lately."

She looked over at him, her eyes full of compassion. "You never even had a chance with your father, did you?"

Wondering where that observation had come from, he said, "Nope. But I'm okay with that. Well, actually I'm not okay with that, but I've learned to live with it." He drove off the exit ramp and headed for the country road that would take them into the rocks and hills and, he hoped, a cool spot to rest. "In fact," he added as he parked the truck and turned to face her, "I've been thinking about trying to find my daddy. I've never actually searched. Maybe it's time I do some digging into my own past." He turned toward her. "Maybe you could help me with that."

"I don't know about that," Anna said, shock echoing through her words as she whipped around to stare at him. "I mean, do you think that would be wise, trying to find him now?"

David sensed the fear in her words. Maybe she didn't want him to be disappointed. "I don't know," he said with a shrug, his fingers drumming on the steering wheel. "But it could help me to get on with things. I feel as if I'm in limbo, always wondering and waiting. I'm tired of wondering. I'm tired of being caught up in the past."

She didn't say anything, but the look of concern on her face told him she didn't like the idea. Or maybe she just didn't want to help him.

"Let's drop that subject for now, okay?" he said

as he got out of the truck and came around to open her door. "Right now, we're just going to relax."

At first she just sat in the truck, staring out at the trees and water. Then she finally turned to him. "I do believe *that* is a good idea. But only for a little while, okay?"

"Okay." David helped her out of the truck then grabbed an old army blanket from the tool box in the back. "I think you'll like this spot, Anna."

Anna watched David wading a few feet away in the clear, shallow waters just off the rocky shore of Lake Austin. She sat and enjoyed just being with him. He'd taken off his button-up shirt and dress shoes and stripped down to his crisp white T-shirt, then rolled up his dress pants.

Now he looked up at her and waved a hand for her to come into the water. "What are you waiting for?"

Anna laughed then leaned back on the blanket. The air was cooler here in the Highland Lakes area, where the Colorado ran into one of the many man-made lakes set up as reservoirs all the way to the gulf. A nice breeze lifted through the nearby Spanish oaks and piñon pines. She took off her sandals then started rolling up her own dark pants, thankful that she'd worn a sleeveless blue top underneath her suit jacket.

Getting up, she moved barefoot down the lime-stone slope toward the water. *I can do this,* she told herself. *I can be here with David and enjoy myself in spite of all my worries and doubts.* He needs me now. And I need him.

Though she'd been hesitant to spend time with him away from work, after the heartbreak of Brandon's grief, her heart ached for this kind of quiet intimacy. Not sure how she could dissuade him from digging up the past, however, she wondered if she should tell Trisha this latest. Maybe if she did, Trisha would save David all that trouble by telling him the truth. But that might end Anna's relationship with David. *Dear God, help me. Tell me what to do.*

"Stop frowning and come on into the lake," David called, sending up an arc of sparkling water through the air to entice her. "It feels great."

And he looked great, standing there with water up to his calves. Ann took a deep breath then decided to let go of all her troubles for a few precious minutes. "Oh, all right. I'm coming."

An hour later, they both fell across the blanket laughing and wet. Anna lay on her back, the cool breeze of the coming dusk moving over her moist skin as she stared across the water at a high limestone ridge covered with mountain laurel and purple sage. "That was fun even if I did probably ruin these pants forever."

David sat back, a broad grin on his face. "Next time, we'll bring bathing suits."

Anna hoped there would be a next time, but she couldn't help but feel a dark cloud falling across the sky. "Summer will be over soon."

He nodded then glanced out toward the crystal-blue water. "And I'll have to get serious about work again."

Anna wanted to reach out and touch a hand to his

wet hair, but she held back, content for now just to look at him. "Will you fly helicopters again, David?"

He nodded. "I'll finish out my stint as a warrant officer, probably behind a desk. Then I'm thinking about applying to fly EMT helicopters at the Prairie Springs Medical Center or maybe the big hospital in Austin. If I stay here, that is."

Anna's heart did a strange little protest. "You might not?"

He turned then, his dark eyes washing over her with longing as he drawled out a loaded question. "That depends. Want me to stay?"

How did she answer that? *Yes, I'd love you to stay. But Trisha is your half sister and you might not be able to handle that.*

"Anna? I need to know."

She looked away, trying to gain control of her erratic emotions. But his hand on her chin brought her head back around. "Anna?"

Anna sat up then brought her hand over his and moved it onto her cheek. "I can't make you stay here just for me. It wouldn't be fair."

"And why not?" He kissed her fingers, each feathery touch sending shivers throughout her system. "Why wouldn't that be fair?"

Anna tried to think of a good reason, but his touch was causing her to lose her resolve. "Well...you've seen me in action. I work all the time. I should be working right now. And soon, you'll be back on a daily routine, too."

"I could find time for you," he said, his eyes as rich and lush as the bottom of a dark spring. He leaned close. "I'd make time for you."

Before Anna could explain why she didn't want him to pin all his hopes on her, David tugged her close and held her a breath away. "Anna? You're running out of excuses and I'm running out of patience." Just to prove that to her, he touched his lips to hers in a gentle kiss.

Anna told herself to stop this, but the warmth of his lips on hers only reinforced the warmth inside her heart. David was a good man, so honorable and so dedicated. He'd never hurt her. How could she hurt him?

She pulled back to stare up at him. "David—"

"No more excuses," he said. "Let's try something different. Let's go on a real date, okay? The date I keep promising."

She must have nodded, because his eyes lit up. "I'll take you to that fancy-pants fund-raiser Trisha keeps nagging me about—"

Shock radiated throughout Anna's system, bringing her out of her daze. "Trisha? What do you mean?"

He looked sheepish but he held her there. "She… uh…wants me to be your date. But I don't care what she wants. I really want to take you, okay?"

Anna tried again to clear the fog inside her brain. "Trisha asked you to take me to the fund-raiser?"

"She didn't ask me. More like—she gave us her blessing."

"I'll just bet she did!" Anna got up, anger burning

the warmth she'd felt into a white-hot heat. "Trisha doesn't make decisions for me."

David shot up to grab her arm. "You're right. It's not for Trisha to decide. I'd take you with or without her approval. But I have to admit trying to be with you works a whole lot better without her breathing down my neck."

Anna turned to look at him, her heart breaking with this treachery Trisha and she had created. "Oh, David, I'm so sorry. I can't believe she forced you to do this—"

He pulled her into his arms. "Nobody forced me, Anna. I don't have to be convinced. Trust me, this is about you and me, Anna, and how we feel."

With that, he kissed her again, showing her exactly how he could overcome all obstacles. Then he lifted his head and pushed a hand through her hair. "Just tell me yes, okay. Just for one night?"

Anna couldn't stop the pounding of her heart. Just for one night. "Yes. Yes, David, you can escort me to the fund-raiser. There, how's that? Think Trisha will leave both of us alone now?"

"She'd better," he said with a big grin. Then he picked Anna up to swing her around in circles, kissing her all over again.

Finally, when they were both out of breath, he stopped then turned her toward the west. "This is what I wanted you to see."

The sun was setting over the hill country, its rays painting the trees and rocks and water in shades of burnished gold and rose-tinted mauve that made the surrounding countryside look like a cache of precious jewels. "Isn't it beautiful?"

"It is," Anna said as she stood in front of him, the warmth of having him near making her feel safe and secure again. "It is." She pivoted to hug him close. "Thank you for making such a sad day so much better."

He kissed her again just as the sun fell behind the hills. "It was my pleasure."

Two hours later, Anna pulled her Jeep into the driveway of the elegant beige brick ranch house Trisha had inherited. As the Texans liked to say, she had a bone to pick with her best friend.

Her knock on the door was fast and swift, but when Trisha opened it, Anna's anger evaporated. Trisha's eyes were red-rimmed and swollen.

"What's wrong?" Anna asked as she swept into the entryway.

Trisha pushed at her long hair then gathered her terry robe around her. "I'm all alone, Anna. That's what's wrong. I just feel so alone sometimes."

"You had another fight with Nick?"

"No, but he's out of town. He had to go to Dallas on business. And I couldn't get in touch with you." She shrugged as she motioned Anna into the spacious den where her father's big leather armchair still held a prominent spot by the fireplace. "I'm not good at Saturday nights all by myself."

"I'm sorry. I turned off my cell." While Anna's

sympathy for her friend's loneliness transcended her anger, she had to be honest with Trisha. Maybe it would jar Trisha into doing the right thing.

"It's okay," Trisha said with a sniff. "I need to get a life anyway."

"You sure do," Anna replied, deciding she'd been Trisha's enabler long enough. Maybe a bit of tough love would shake her friend up. "And you need to stop interfering with mine."

Shocked, Trisha whirled to glare at her. "Excuse me?"

Anna sat down on the comfy white couch. "Trisha, you know I love you but you can't go behind my back asking David to take me out. I'm not a charity case, after all."

"Oh, that." Trisha waved a hand in the air. "I was just trying to help. I can see how things are with you two, but you're so afraid to take that next step. I just gave David a little nudge."

"But don't you see that by doing so you've put me in a very awkward position? I can't let myself become any more involved with David, not until you tell him the truth."

Trisha's pout returned. "I'm not sure I can ever do that."

Anna's frustration matched the pout on Trisha's face. "Well, then I can't take that next step—as you put it—with David. I'm going on this one date with him only because I'll be so busy that night anyway, we won't get to spend much time together. But after that, I'm going to have to break things off with him. I can't be with him and keep this from him. It's not right and it's not fair."

Trisha moaned then hit her hands against her chair. "But it's my decision whether or not even to tell him. I know it's my father's dying request, but I have to find the right time…"

"It has everything to do with us. This *mess* is his life," Anna said, getting up to leave. "And this mess is interfering with my life now." Feeling contrite for the rage that had built inside her, she softened her voice. "Look, honey, I know how hard this is for you, but I believe that once David has time to think about it, he'll be okay. I think he'll be better than okay because he'll know the whole story at last. At least I'm praying for that." When Trisha didn't respond, she added, "Trisha, he's thinking about looking into his past, as in, trying to find out who his father was. And he has the resources right here on post to do that. Wouldn't you rather he hears this from you?"

Trisha put a hand to her mouth. "Oh, I don't know what to do. I just don't know."

"Yes, you do," Anna said, reaching out to take Trisha's hand. "You have to do this. And not just so I can go to the stupid ball with the prince."

That made Trisha grin even though she looked scared and unsure. "Well, at least I got that part right. So…you are going with him?"

Anna giggled, for a moment feeling fifteen again. "Yes, I am, since you two have been passing notes about me behind my back. Isn't high school so much fun?"

"It's not adolescent to want my best friend to be happy," Trisha retorted with a grimace. "So what are you wearing, anyway?"

Anna panicked then. "Oh, my. I have no idea! I hadn't even thought about that. Mother tried to convince me to buy this horrid dress the other day, but other than that I haven't had time to worry about it."

Trisha perked up immediately. "We can make a trip into Austin or better yet, Houston or Dallas. We can do Neiman's—"

"Whoa," Anna said, getting up again. "I don't have time to do Neiman's. I'll be lucky if I can run into the local department store on Veterans Boulevard."

"No." Trisha looked as if she might faint. "You will not wear anything from that hideous store, Anna."

"I do wear things from that hideous store, Trisha."

"Not on this night," Trisha retorted. "I might not know how to deal with my secret half brother, but I do know fashion. And you, my dear Anna, are going to be the belle of the ball."

"Oh, great." Anna didn't know whether to run and hide or just to relax and get through this night. Then a thought struck her. "Trisha, I'll let you help me with a dress and we'll get through the fund-raiser. But after that, you have to talk to David, okay?"

Trisha looked serious for a minute then nodded. "After the fund-raiser, I promise. Really, Anna. I'll tell David everything once we get through this night."

One more week, Anna thought as she headed back home. One more week before David found out the truth. She only hoped he could forgive Trisha for withholding this information. And she hoped he could see it in his heart to forgive her, too.

Chapter Thirteen

Anna knocked on Olga's door to say good-night.

"Come in," her mother called in her singsong voice.

Anna opened the door and found her mother sitting at her vanity holding a framed picture of Anna's father. "Hello, Mommy. Or rather, good night."

Olga motioned Anna in. "Not just yet, Anna-bug." She rubbed a hand over the image of Feador Terenkov. "I've had your father on my mind today."

Anna sat down on the plush skirted footstool near her mother's chair, her gaze touching on her father's debonair image. "That's understandable. Sergeant Matthews's death has stirred up a lot of emotions around here."

Olga nodded. "He was such a good man. So dedicated. And to leave his wife and son too young." She gave an eloquent shrug. "We'll find our answers one day, Anna."

"Will we?" Anna longed to tell her mother all her troubles, but tonight Olga looked so drained and tired that Anna had to remember her mother put on a great act. Even upbeat, bubbly Olga sometimes let the weight of this war crush her resolve.

"I suppose you'll always miss Papa, won't you?"

Olga nodded then carefully put down the oval silver frame. "Yes, always."

Anna couldn't help but wonder though. "Mommy, are you really interested in Reverend Fields, or are you just trying to find a companion of sorts?"

Olga put a hand to her throat, her smile serene and full of secrets. "It's very strange, isn't it, seeing your mother flirting with another man—and a minister at that."

"I have to admit it's a bit disturbing," Anna replied, her smile indulgent. "I haven't handled it very well, but I've never seen you even look toward anyone since Papa died."

"There you go again," Olga said, reaching over to pat Anna's arm. "You called him Papa. Whenever you call me Mommy and your father Papa, I know you're having some troubles of your own."

"And you're trying to shift the topic from you to me, I believe. You still haven't answered my question."

"That's because I don't know the true answer. I only know that whenever I look at Reverend Frank, I get goose bumps. Silly, but that's the way it is."

Anna nodded, deciding her mother could keep up

this word play for hours if she didn't let it go. "I guess we need answers for a lot of things these days."

Olga stood up as if she'd just realized she wasn't putting on that good front she liked to present to the world. "Of course we'll find all of our answers one way or another, whether we like the answers or not. God knows why the world spins the way it does. We're just here for the ride."

"And what if that ride gets to be too much?" Anna asked. "Sometimes I feel as if I'd like to step off and just rest."

Olga touched her fingers to the fringe of Anna's long bangs. "You're tired, darling. You need a nice cup of tea and a good night's sleep. You work too hard and you take every burden onto your shoulders."

"I haven't been at work over the last few hours," Anna admitted. "I was with David."

"Oh, I see." Olga's smile filled with hope and maybe a bit of trepidation. "A fine young man, that one."

"He is a good man." Anna struggled with her secrets. "And he's kind to me."

"So why the long face?" Olga asked. "Do you have feelings for David?"

She wasn't ready to tell her mother that she was in love with David. "I think I do. We're going to the COTD fund-raiser together next weekend."

"How delightful," Olga said, clasping her hands together. "You need to find a decent dress."

"You and Trisha, always worried about how I dress." While Anna's tone was sharp, her smile belied the harshness of her words. "But I certainly don't have much time to worry about the latest fashions."

"Well, someone has to stay on you for that very reason," Olga said as she reached for her favorite lotion and rubbed it all over her hands and arms. The scent of gardenia filled the big room. She reached for Anna's hands, rubbing lotion over her fingers, a smile on her face. "This is about more than a dress, isn't it, Anna-bug?"

Anna nodded. "I have a problem. Can I tell you something in confidence?"

"Of course," Olga replied, her eyes wide with worry. "What is it?"

Anna let out a long sigh. "Trisha found out recently that…that the commander had an affair before Trisha was born and that she has an older half brother because of it."

Olga dropped her hands in her lap. "Oh, my goodness. I can't believe—"

"Neither could I." Anna explained the stipulations of Commander Morrison's letter. "He didn't want his wife to know so he never told anyone. The letter was his way of trying to make amends, I think. Now Trisha has to tell her brother the truth. He has no idea, but he needs to know."

"I think that would be best, yes," Olga said, nodding. "Where is this long-lost brother anyway?"

"He's right here in Prairie Springs," Anna said. "Mother, it's David Ryland."

Olga held her hands to her face, her mouth forming

a silent O of shock. "Goodness, darling. I would have never dreamed in a million years." Then she let out a little huff. "Your David. That is amazing."

"Yes, my David." Anna shook her head. "So you see my dilemma. I'm falling for the man who just happens to be my best friend's half brother. What will he think of me when he finds out the truth? When he finds out that I knew all along that he was Trisha's brother?"

Olga did a little tsk-tsk in her throat, her eyes wandering around the room as she tried to think of how to advise Anna. "Well, I can't speak for the man, but if David knows you the way he should know you, he'll understand that you weren't at liberty to reveal what you knew. Trisha told you this in confidence so he should understand that, don't you think?"

"I hope," Anna said, getting up. "But…he's very bitter about never knowing his father. This could bring Trisha and David together, or it could destroy David completely, not to mention what it will do to our relationship. He trusts me, Mommy. I don't know what to do."

"Take it to the Lord in prayer," Olga suggested. "That's all you can do until you see how David is going to react. You can't tell him this. Trisha has to be the one. But you can be the one who's waiting there for him after the truth is out. He'll need a good friend then."

"She's going to tell him after the fund-raiser," Anna said. "Trisha can't deal with the stress of getting this event together and telling him the truth right now. And frankly, I don't think I can, either."

Olga pressed her hands into her lap. "And you're having a hard time with the deceit, either way."

"Yes, I am. It's not right. I don't want to hurt David, but I have to honor Trisha's wishes on this."

Olga got up and came to Anna, taking her into her arms for a long mother's hug. "If David really has strong feelings for you, he should be able to get past this, darling. You have to believe that." Then her mother leaned back to give her a stern look. "And Anna-bug, you can't use this as an excuse, thinking to just let David go. You need someone special in your life. You have to hold out hope. And sometimes, you have to fight for that hope."

Anna held to her mother's words as she got ready for bed. *Please Lord, let my mother be right. Please allow David to understand my motives. Please don't let me hurt him. And please allow my heart to open wide enough to accept this overwhelming love.*

He hurt all over.

David stopped running to take in deep gulps of air. "When did I get so out of shape?"

Brandon stopped beside him, jogging in place as he faced David. "Maybe you're just getting soft around the edges."

"Maybe," David replied, glad that the boy had agreed to go running with him this morning. "What about you? How're you feeling?"

Brandon gave him a teenaged shrug. "Fine." Then he glanced around to make sure they were alone on the paved walking path around the park on the edge of town. "I'm worried about my mom, though. I don't know how to talk to her. I mean, she cries when she thinks I'm not looking. And when I am around, she tries to baby me. Only, I'm not a baby."

David's heart ached for the Matthews family. "Want me to go by and visit with her?"

"What good would that do?" Brandon asked, his hands on his hips. "It won't bring my dad back."

"No, but it might help her to see that you're the man of the family now. And I hope you continue to act like a man."

"I'm trying," Brandon said. "If I can just make it through school, then I can join up."

"What? Join up?" David's mind went back in time. Hadn't he done the very same thing, just to ir-ritate his mother, just to get back at her? "Do you think that's smart?"

"Why not? If it was good enough for my daddy—"

David took another breath as he stepped closer to Brandon. "Don't do it for the wrong reasons. Serving in the military is hard on a good day, but if you get stationed in a war zone, it becomes very real. You need to have your head together or…"

"Or I'll get myself killed?" Brandon gave him a scowl. "Are you saying he didn't have his head to-gether? Or maybe he was just in the wrong place at the wrong time? Are you saying my dad—?"

Biting back a sharp retort, David put a hand on Brandon's shoulder. "Your father was a brave man who was trying to do his job. That's the way it works in the army. We try to get the job done."

"That's what I plan on doing one day, then," Brandon said, his expression stony. "I plan to finish the job my daddy started."

David couldn't argue with Brandon's need to seek justice, but he hoped the boy wouldn't get hotheaded on him and cop an attitude. "Okay, fine. Just think long and hard before you make any decisions. You've got a few years to get this straight in your mind."

"My mind is made up," Brandon said. "I'm going to join up when I graduate from high school. Right now, I'm just worried about my mother."

"I'll go and see her," David said. "That's a promise. And you know you're in my prayers."

"I don't need promises and prayers," Brandon shot over his shoulder. "I just need her to feel better." With that he was off and running again. "I'm going home."

David watched the boy sprint away, hurting even more now than when he'd gotten up this morning with his mind on Anna and how much he'd enjoyed being with her at Lake Austin last weekend. His physical aches could be chalked up to doing too much work yesterday afternoon in the old garage behind the COTD offices. He'd purposely worked out there for the last couple of days just to take his mind off Brandon's situation and his own need to find out who his father was. But he'd mainly stayed busy to keep his mind off how he was falling for Anna. So while Olga and her pretty, mysterious daughter had spent most of their spare time at Brandon's house trying to console his mother and help her with the paperwork and other red tape involved in being a military widow, David had taken a long time to work and think. He needed so many answers.

Only, he still didn't have any. He cared about Anna but he sensed hesitancy in her each time they were together. Maybe she was just concerned about work and how having a relationship would affect that. Or maybe her fears ran deeper. Was Anna afraid to love any man?

David could appreciate that kind of fear, but he wanted Anna to see that her heart was safe with him. On the one hand, he told himself not to rush headlong into a relationship before he'd become fully settled back home. But he didn't want to listen to that voice—David knew he cared about Anna. He just wasn't sure what he had to offer her. That old self-doubt kept kicking him in the gut. How could he ever hope to fit into Anna's world, when he'd never fit in here before?

"I don't know, Lord," David mumbled to himself as he turned to run back up Veterans Boulevard. "I just don't know."

When he heard a horn honking, he stopped to glance out onto the street. Trisha Morrison sat at the traffic light, grinning in her top-down sports car. "Looking good, soldier."

David jogged out onto the empty street. "You're up early for a socialite."

Did he see a bit of hurt in her bright eyes at that remark? "I have a million things to do before Saturday," she said, tossing her long hair out of the way. "Only a few days now before the big event. Hope you found your dress uniform."

David gave her wink then said in an exaggerated drawl, "I might not have a lot of flash and dash, ma'am, but I do believe I can manage to clean up real nice for your fancy shindig. This ain't my first rodeo."

Trisha laughed as the traffic light changed. "Wait until you see Anna in her dress."

With that, she waved as she shifted gears and took off, leaving David to wonder just what she had up her sleeve. Then he had another thought. Trisha knew a lot of important people in this town and her father had once been the post commander. A few days ago, she would have been the last person he'd have turned to for help. But Trisha wasn't all fluff. He'd seen that the night she'd sat playing a board game with little Ali. Maybe she'd be willing to help him do a little research into finding out more about his own father.

Two days later Trisha rushed into Anna's office, her gaze darting here and there. Scanning the waiting area where several clients sat, she asked, "Is David here?"

"No," Anna said, holding her finger on the file she'd been reading. The phone rang across the way in Caitlyn's office and she heard Caitlyn's crisp voice as she talked to someone on the line about their upcoming fall clothing sale. "David hasn't been in much this week. He's spending a lot of time with Brandon, I think. Why do you ask?"

"I don't want him to hear what I'm about to say," Trisha replied as she closed the door of Anna's office. While they could see through the glass panel, their voices would be more muted with the door closed. Trisha waved to Caitlyn, then turned back to Anna. "I don't want anyone to hear this."

"What's going on?" Anna asked, her heart stopping. She didn't think she could handle any more drama this week.

"Anna, he called me last night. And you won't believe what he asked me to do?"

Knowing she wouldn't like this, Anna nodded. "Go on."

"He wants me to help him track down his father! *His* father, Anna. Can you believe that?"

Anna put her head against her hand then lifted her gaze toward Trisha. "Why you?" But she thought she could figure that one out on her own. She'd declined helping him, had even suggested finding his father might not be a good idea. So he'd been desperate enough to turn to Trisha, of all people. Things were just going from bad to worse.

"He thinks I have a lot of connections since *my* father was the post commander. Wait until he finds out just how connected I really am!"

"What did you tell him?"

"I told him I couldn't help him until later, maybe next week after this ball is over. I mean, that's when I plan telling him everything anyway."

Thinking of the hope David had probably put on this request, not to mention how he'd swallowed his pride to ask Trisha, she asked, "You're not going to actually do that, are you?"

Trisha shook her head, her dark eyes full of resolve. Her cell went off. Digging it out of her purse, she checked the call then ignored it. "No, I'm not. I'm just going to sit down with him and tell him the truth. I can't go on like this anymore. David's a nice guy and well…I don't think I'll mind having him for a brother."

Anna didn't know whether to be glad or concerned. "Mother always says we might not like the answers God grants us when we pray, and in this case, I'm torn."

Trisha looked confused. "But you've been advising me to tell him the truth."

"Yes, and I want you to do that. I'm just dreading his reaction." She leaned forward, her voice low. "Trisha, you have to consider that he might not be ready to play big brother. He has a lot of bitterness toward his father, not to mention a lot of anger about being an outcast when he was growing up here. I don't want you to be disappointed."

"I know," Trisha said. "And I'm sure he'll hate me at first. I'll just have to deal with that when it comes.

I plan on going to a lawyer to divide father's estate with David, if he'll allow that. I have a feeling he'll tell me no, but I'm going to try anyway. What else can I do? David has every right to his inheritance, same as me. He doesn't know it, but he's actually pretty wealthy now. I owe him that much, at least."

"You're right," Anna said, admiring Trisha for having reached that generous conclusion.

Trisha got up, shuffling through her tote bag as her phone beeped again. "I can't think about this right now. I've got a meeting with the caterers and I need to check the sound system at the country club. Plus, I have the final fitting on my dress and—" She stopped, her gaze slamming into Anna's. "Oh, Anna, I'm so sorry I dragged you into this. I won't tell David that you knew."

Anna shook her head. "You won't have to. He'll figure that out right away, I'm afraid."

She didn't tell Trisha that she was also afraid she would lose David forever when he did find out. Watching Trisha rush out the door, she silently asked, *Oh, Lord, help me. What have I done?*

"Everything okay?" Caitlyn called from across the hall.

Anna looked up with a soft smile. "Same as usual. Trisha is in a tizzy about Saturday night. I guess we all are." She grabbed her files and her bag. "In fact, I need to check on a few things myself. I have to make sure the table arrangements are exactly what we requested and I want to go over the seating chart."

Caitlyn waved a hand. "Go ahead. I'll cover things."

Anna made sure the two remaining clients were being served, checked on the volunteers putting together the annual report for Saturday's patron dinner then rushed to her Jeep. Maybe if she just rode around for a while…

She turned on the back porch steps to find David walking toward her.

"Hey, beautiful, where you going in such a hurry?"

Chapter Fourteen

"David, how are you?"

"I'm okay." He shifted on his boots then looked back up at her. "Actually, I'm not okay. But I'm working on getting better."

A deep current of longing and understanding shot through Anna. "Is there something I can do to help?"

He shook his head. "No. I need to work through this myself. I think I just need to get back to my daily routine. I've got too much time on my hands."

Anna leaned against her Jeep, the late-August heat quickly zapping her energy. "You needed this time, though. From what I hear from dealing with returning soldiers and their families, this is a time of readjustment for everyone."

His gaze locked with hers. "I don't have a family, Anna."

Wishing she could drop through the earth, Anna purposely put on a smile so he wouldn't see the sympathy in her eyes. "What about your mother? I'm sure she really misses you."

"I'm going to see her next week."

Anna's heart hit a pounding beat, drumming through her pulse while she tried to stay calm. Next week. Everything would change then. "I guess you do need to see her while you still have some leave time."

"Yeah. I've been putting it off long enough. I want to ask her about my father. And maybe this time she'll level with me." He let out a long sigh. "I've been struggling with this my whole life, you know. And now that I'm back here, I've realized I can't move past it. I think that's why I asked to come back here. I want this struggle to be over." Then he stepped close. "Especially since I've met you."

She tried to make her tone light, but her heart felt like a lead weight. "What do I have to do with it?"

"Everything," he said. "I want to be the kind of man you deserve, Anna. And I can't be that man until I get this out of my head. I mean, that is the reason you keep stalling out on me, right? I can be so bitter at times and I'm tired of being bitter. I have a lot to be thankful for and now I can see that."

"David—"

"Don't say anything, Chief." He took one of her hands in his. "Let's just look forward to this special night coming up. Let's pretend everything is all right and that I am that man—the man who can make you happy. I want that for just one night."

He kissed her on the cheek then started walking

backwards toward the house. "I promised Caitlyn I'd help out with some of the client paperwork today. I'd better get in there."

Anna watched him walking away, her heart crushed against her chest. She'd come so close to telling him the truth. *David, you are that man,* she wanted to shout. *You are so much like your father.*

Anna tried to catch her breath. All this time, she'd been so worried about David finding out the truth, not only because of what it would do to both Trisha and him, but mostly because she wanted David to care about her. She didn't want to disappoint him. But the obstacles keeping them apart went so much deeper than that. She'd closed herself off from a life outside of work, simply because her grief and guilt over her father's death had been the driving force in her need to help others. And David had shut down because he'd never had an opportunity to meet his father. And he still hadn't managed to rise above his upbringing even though he was a true hero.

"How can he think he's not good enough?" she wondered as she cranked the Jeep and hoped the feeble air-conditioning would kick in. "Can't he see that he's a good man?" David had flaws, but then who didn't? Anna was willing to forgive those flaws. And she prayed he'd forgive hers.

But apparently he couldn't forgive himself for being born out of wedlock. He couldn't forgive himself for not being good enough to merit his father's attention.

And that meant David didn't think he was truly worthy of God's attention, either. Or anyone else's for that matter. Including hers.

Anna sat in her hot, humid Jeep, her prayers echoing inside the humming of the rattling air-conditioning. "Dear Father, help David to see the good in himself. Help him to know that he is doing the best he can."

And help me to get through this and stand firm against his anger.

"Stand up straight."

"Mother, please." Anna rolled her eyes at Olga's frown but she did as she was told. Staring at her reflection in the standing mirror inside her mother's spacious, frilly bedroom, Anna couldn't believe how she looked. "Is this really me?"

Olga, dressed in mint-green chiffon that floated in layers around her, nodded as she clasped her hands together. "It's you, my Anna-bug. Oh, your father would be so proud."

Anna whirled in a crush of blue watered-silk taffeta. "Do you think so?"

"I know so," Olga said, making last-minute adjustments to Anna's sleeveless, bead-trimmed dress. "You are so beautiful. David will be beside himself."

"David— Oh, look at the time. He'll be here any minute."

"You're ready," Olga announced, satisfied with the tiny diamonds shimmering in Anna's ears. "Your hair is perfect and the jewelry is just right, not too gaudy."

"We wouldn't want gaudy," Anna said, smiling at her upswept hair. Trisha had left her long bangs loose to fall against Anna's temple like a shield and Anna planned to use that shield. "Trisha did a good job on me, though, didn't she?"

"She did indeed." Olga whirled, the scent of gardenia following her as she grabbed her gold evening bag. "Now, I'm off. I'll see you there."

"Thanks, Mother," Anna said. "For everything."

Olga turned to smile over at her. "Don't you worry about anything, Anna-bug. David is going to love you."

Anna waved goodbye to her mother then turned to stare at her reflection in the mirror. "I love him already, Mother. But I'm not sure that's enough."

He couldn't get enough of just looking at her.

David watched as Anna seemed to float across the room. Her dress was long and an iridescent blue that shimmered like a sapphire each time she moved. Her hair was piled up on her head in what might have been a severe style except for those adorable long bangs falling across one eye. Her smile was million-dollar quality as she greeted patrons and contributors to her cause. She knew how to handle this ritzy crowd.

David had seen her vivid beauty the minute she'd come sweeping down the stairs to greet him earlier. Now he could see the vivid contrast between their lives. Anna might have been shy in high school, but she was in her element here amongst some of the richest people in town, while he stood here in the corner, sweating in his crisp dress blues. How could he possibly expect someone like Anna to want to be with someone like him?

Their different lifestyles had become obvious at the formal sit-down dinner earlier. Anna could barely enjoy her meal, since people kept stopping by their table to talk to her and wish her well. But somehow, she'd managed to include him in almost every conversation. The party should bring in the funds she needed because it seemed everyone in town loved Anna.

Where did that leave him? While the patrons had been polite, thanking him for doing his duty, David still felt like a bronc rider at a ballet. Way out of his element.

He felt a tap on his shoulder and turned to find Chaplain Steve and Caitlyn grinning at him. Caitlyn's golden-brown hair shimmered to match her glittering brown ball gown.

"Hi, David," Caitlyn said. "How's it going?"

"Pretty good. How are y'all doing?"

Chaplain Steve's smile was just for Caitlyn. "I feel like a million bucks myself. We've been enjoying the band."

"I didn't know he could waltz," Caitlyn admitted.

"It's a nice party," David replied, wondering where Anna had gotten to. "I might have to try the two-step myself."

"I can guarantee Anna would love that," Caitlyn

said with another grin. "We're off in search of some punch and food. They've put out the dessert buffet."

David laughed. "After that big meal, I don't know where you'll put dessert."

"For a small woman, she has a big appetite," Steve said as Caitlyn tugged him away with a giggle.

David watched as they whispered in each other's ears, envying the way they seemed perfect for each other.

"Don't look so glum, soldier."

This time it was Dr. Nora Blake and she was not giggling. But David saw the twinkle in her eyes.

"Hey, Doc. How's Ali?"

"Progressing very well," the attractive blonde said. Her hair was pulled up in a very severe chignon and her white dress followed her tall slender curves with tailor-made precision. "He tires out a lot so he has to take naps and rest in bed most days, but we're watching him very closely. I hope to perform the surgery in a few weeks, barring any setbacks."

"That's reassuring." David saw Anna coming toward him and breathed a sigh of relief.

"Don't worry about Ali. We're going to get him patched up and back in shape as soon as we can." The doctor waved to someone across the room. "Excuse me, David. It was nice to see you."

David watched her walk away, wondering how she'd managed to become a doctor instead of a runway model.

"Hey, stop checking out Dr. Nora," Anna said with a wink.

David pulled her close. "I only have eyes for one woman in this room, trust me."

Her smile told him she liked that. "I hope that woman is me."

"You got that right, Chief. Wanna get dessert?"

"Maybe." Anna glanced around then groaned. "Oh, goodness. My mother is determined to make Reverend Fields notice her. Let's go and try to rescue him."

She took David by the hand, dragging him across the crowded ballroom until she was beside Olga and the minister. "Mother, want to get some dessert and go out on the terrace?"

Olga turned with a beaming smile. "No, darling. I'm stuffed. That dinner was excellent. Trisha outdid herself with the steak medallions and rosemary potatoes, don't you agree, Reverend?"

Reverend Fields looked like a trapped rabbit. David felt sorry for the man. The minister had done his duty by dressing in a nice tux, but he looked as out of place as a cowboy at a cotillion. David could understand the good reverend's pain.

"How's it going, Reverend?" David asked after Anna nudged him with her elbow.

"Not so good," Franklin said, his tone dry as he watched the crowd. "I hate these things."

"Now, Reverend, you know this is for a good cause," Olga replied, her bubbling personality going into overdrive. "And we're having fun."

"I believe in good causes, Mrs. Terenkov, but I don't like having to get all gussied up to be a part of one of these formal events."

Olga giggled again. "But you look so handsome in your tux, don't you think so, Anna?"

"Very nice," Anna said, this time nudging her mother.

"What is it?" Olga asked, clearly not taking the hint. "Do you need me for something, darling?"

Anna leaned close, but David heard the warning in her whisper to her mother. "I need you to stop making a spectacle of yourself."

"Anna!" Olga looked shocked then hurt. "What are you talking about?"

Anna raised her voice above the music but the music ended just as she spoke. "Stop flirting with the pastor, Mother."

Reverend Fields heard that one. As did several people standing nearby.

Olga turned a bright pink while Anna put a hand to her mouth, her eyes going wide. "I'm sorry."

Reverend Fields put his own discomfort aside and said, "No harm done, Anna. I don't mind getting your mother something cool to drink. Come on, Mrs. Terenkov. Let's find that punch bowl."

With that, he extended his arm to Olga. She took it, but she'd lost a lot of the luster from her eyes. Tossing Anna a hurt look over her shoulder, Olga marched away with the minister.

"That didn't go so well," Anna said as she

looked up at David. "Can we get out of here for just a few minutes?"

"I'd like nothing better," David said as he escorted her out a side door to the coolness of the country club terrace. "Want to go to the river or Lake Austin?"

She sighed then shook her head. "I can't leave. Let's just get some fresh air. I need a break."

David didn't argue with that. He'd wanted her to himself all evening. But now that he had her to himself, he wasn't sure what to say. So he remained silent.

"Is something wrong?" she asked, sounding fragile while her smile remained courageous.

"Nothing that can't be fixed with this." He pulled her close and kissed her. When he lifted his head, the music was back. "Want to dance?" he asked, holding her at arm's length as the slow, romantic song drifted out into the night.

Anna nodded. "I'd love that."

Anna loved being in David's arms. He looked great in his dress uniform and she'd been proud to have him on her arm as they'd entered the country club. Although he'd been quiet during dinner, his presence beside her had given her the confidence she needed to get through this night. Nervous energy had her jittery and the smile she'd worn all night had given her a headache. And she'd hurt her mother, something she hadn't set out to do. But now, being out here alone with him more than made up for all of that.

As the music ended, he released her then stared down at her. "Finally. I've wanted to do that all night."

Anna smiled, her hands settling on his shoulders. "Kiss me or dance with me?"

"Both. But mostly I just wanted you to myself."

"Has it been that bad?"

"Nah. I knew I wouldn't get to spend much time with you, but at least I've been able to enjoy watching you do your thing all night. I think I could watch you forever."

"You're sweet. Trisha and Mother insisted I get all dressed up. I usually wear something much more sedate to this affair."

"You go through this every year?"

"Like clockwork. We need the funding to keep our doors open."

"I wish I could do more, but on my salary—"

"You've done a lot. And you've made me realize I need to take time for myself…to enjoy some of the perks of being single."

"That has perks?"

"It does when I'm standing in your arms."

"I sure like the sound of that."

Anna laughed then let out a breath of frustration. "I shouldn't have said that to my mother. I'm just so worried. She's never looked at another man since my father's death. And now all she can talk about is our minister and how she thinks they're 'made for each other.'"

"She deserves a second chance, I reckon. Even if she did wait about twenty years to take that chance."

"I suppose so. And she's taking a big risk, going after a man of God. I'm so afraid she'll be crushed by his rejection. Somehow, I can't picture my mother as a minister's wife."

"What's wrong with that? Your mother is still young enough to enjoy life and Reverend Fields might need someone like her in his life, you know, to balance things."

"So you think I'm being unfair to her?"

"I think you're just being cautious. Maybe you don't want her to get hurt, but she has to be lonely and we all know what that's like. It's the same reason Trisha kept warning me off you at first. She's lonely, so she's afraid she'll lose you to someone else. You could be afraid you'll lose your mother, but I don't think that's gonna happen."

"You're right," Anna said, glad to have a different perspective on things. "It's been just the two of us for so long now, I'm probably a bit possessive. I'm going to have a long talk with her later. I'll try not to be so judgmental when we do talk."

"Good idea. I think they're kinda cute together."

"Cute? I wouldn't quite call it that, but something is sure stewing between them."

"How about us?" he asked, holding his thumb to her chin. "Is something stewing between us?"

"I think so," she said with a sigh. "Or I wouldn't be wearing this dress and these shoes."

"I like you whether you're wearing this or not, you know that, right?" He kissed her as she nodded then took her hand as they walked toward the stone banister. "Where's your sidekick Trisha anyway? I haven't seen her all night."

Anna looked out over the golf course and the twinkling lights beside the pool. "She's running around making sure everything goes as planned. She amazes me. Trisha loves this. She's so good at fund-raising because she knows so many people in town."

"Yeah—all the rich people. All the right people." Chaplain Steve suggested I talk to her about tracking down my father. And since I'd already decided to ask her anyway, I did call her. She said maybe after all of this is over. But I'm not so sure I need to involve her."

Anna heard the doubt in his words, a chilling dread curling like mist throughout her system. He would never forgive Trisha or her when he found out the truth.

Hoping to end the subject, she said, "Well, whatever you decide, I hope you find what you're looking for."

"I intend to, one way or another."

Anna had to ask. "But what if you don't like what you find?"

He looked out over the trees and rolling hills. "It won't matter. At least I'll finally know. It's the not knowing that's driving me crazy."

She stood silent for a minute then said, "Isn't it a beautiful night?"

David pulled her back into his arms. "Yes, it is. I wish we were at the river."

"Not in this dress," Anna replied on a giggle.

He stood back to admire her. "You're beautiful. Too beautiful for the likes of me, I think."

"Now, why would you think that?"

He shrugged. "Look at me, Anna. No matter what kind of uniform I wear, I'm still the poor kid who didn't have a father growing up."

"Only if you let that guide your life. Only if you continue to see yourself that way. You're worth more than that, David. And honestly, I don't see how you can expect any more from yourself if that's the image you carry in your heart."

"It's the way people see me. It was that way growing up and now that I'm home, it kind of feels that way again."

"Have any of us treated you unkindly?" she asked, compassion giving her the strength she needed to combat this mighty enemy. "Has anyone here shunned you?"

"No," he said as if it had finally dawned on him. "No, you're right. Everyone has been more than kind to me."

He groaned. "I've made a mess of things, haven't I? I should look for the good but all I see is the bad. Maybe I shouldn't have returned to Prairie Springs. Too many memories."

She touched a hand to his arm. "And yet, you didn't let that stop you from serving your country. You went out and signed up to fight, David, and you came back to face those memories. Don't you see the honor in that?"

He whirled to stare down at her. "I see that I did it for all the wrong reasons. I was trying to live up to this image inside my head. This image of an absent father who didn't care enough to be a part of my life. Now I wonder whether he would have been proud of me. If I don't find out the truth, I'll never know that, will I?"

Anna gave him a resigned nod. "No, and you'll never get past this, either. And I don't see us having a future until you do. I can see the resentment in your eyes when you're with me. You think our lives are different, but I didn't have it any better than you did. I made a new life for myself in a new place. You have to do the same, but in a familiar place. You have to move forward. And if that means finding out things about your father, well, then I guess that's what you need to do."

"Yes, that's exactly what I have to do, and soon."

Anna was about to tell him that his father would have been very proud, when they heard a discreet cough in the shadows. Trisha stepped out, her red dress falling around her ankles. "I can help you with the truth, David. In fact, I think it's time you did know the truth. All of it."

Chapter Fifteen

David looked from Trisha back to Anna. "What's she talking about?"

Anna whirled to her friend. "Trisha, not now—"

"Why wait?" Trisha said, her words shaky but sure, her eyes full of resolve. "I came out here to find you two and I heard you talking about how you don't fit in, David. But you fit in more than you realize." She looked from Anna to him. "You think I'm this shallow socialite born with a silver spoon in her mouth, don't you?"

"Aren't you?" He lifted his hands then let them drop to his side. "That's not a condemnation, it's just a fact of life," he said, his expression shuttered with embarrassment. "Look, Trisha—"

"You don't know the whole story, David. But you should hear it and from me. It's the only way you can get on with your life and it's the only way you'll ever understand mine."

He shook his head. "No, I don't need you to explain your life to me. I get it. I just want to spend some time with Anna, without you standing in the shadows judging me."

"She's right, David," Anna said, her shoulders slumping. "And I guess now is as good a time as any for you to hear the truth—from her."

The look in Anna's eyes floored him. She looked defeated and heartbroken. But her words hit him with all the force of a grenade. He took her hand. "What are you saying? What's the matter?"

Anna looked back at Trisha. "Trisha needs to talk to you about your father."

"Do you know something?" David asked Trisha, hope rising in his heart. "When I asked you for help I didn't expect you to find out anything so soon."

"I know a lot," Trisha said, stepping toward them with her hands clutched together. "As you said, I know all the right people. And I also realize you must have been desperate to come to me for help, since you seem to resent everything I stand for."

David didn't like the expression on her face or the way Anna held her head down, refusing to look at him. "Anna?"

"I'm so sorry, David," Anna said, turning to leave.

He grabbed her arm again, a warning burn going through his stomach with rocket force. "What's going on here?"

"Trisha will tell you," Anna said. "You know where to find me if you need me."

* * *

"Let's go sit down," Trisha said after Anna had left.

"I think I should go after her," David said, clearly unnerved. "I've upset her. And you."

Trisha laughed, but the sound caught in her throat. "No, I'm the one who's upset Anna. She was just being a good friend. She's always been that way."

David gave up trying to read between the lines, but his gut told him he wasn't going to like what he was about to hear. So he sat down on the stone bench with Trisha, away from the sound of music and laughter coming from the open doors of the opulent reception hall. "So…Anna is your go-to girl whenever you're in trouble—a broken fingernail, a torn skirt, a fight with your boyfriend?"

Trisha nodded, silent and still, her hands twisted together in her lap. "I guess you *do* think I'm that shallow."

David instantly regretted his condemning words. "I think you're rich and pampered and privileged and yes, I resent those things. But I didn't mean to hurt you or Anna. That's just something I have to get over."

"Yes, it is. But you're right. I am all of those things. I was blessed to be born to a wonderful set of parents who tried to give me the best of everything. And you weren't so blessed, from what I've heard."

He shook his head, confused about the true sympathy in her eyes. But he didn't want her sympathy. "No, I wasn't but I shouldn't have taken that out on you." Dreading the question, he had to ask it anyway. "So…what do you know about my father?"

Trisha crossed her long legs, her silver sandals twinkling in the moonlight as she wrapped her hands over her knee. Letting out a breath, she said, "I knew him, David. I knew your father. We were very close."

David digested that, holding his shock in check for now. A charge of awareness shot through his system, followed by a sickening numbness. "And how did you know him?"

"Oh, I think you can figure that out," Trisha said, giving him a direct look. "I mean, isn't it obvious? My father was an important man around here before his death. But back when your mother knew him he was a newly commissioned officer. A married officer."

David's heart slammed and shifted with the intensity of rapid-fire bullets. "What are you saying?"

Trisha didn't flinch. "Your mother and my father had an affair before I was born. I'm your half sister. Your shallow, rich, superficial half sister. Welcome to the family."

David couldn't breathe. He stood outside Anna's house, staring up at the light in her window. Commander Davis Morrison, a brigadier general and army hero, was his father.

His father. The words sounded so foreign to David, he couldn't grasp the true meaning. A former post commander was his father. And all those years when David and his mother had lived in a falling-down trailer on the outskirts of town, the man who would one day come back to Fort Bonnell as its leader had lived in a nice stately officer's home on post. And he'd gone on to father a daughter who had become the apple of her daddy's eye. While his illegitimate son suffered a few miles away.

David had often wondered on those long sleepless nights of his adolescence if he'd ever overcome his shame and his inadequacies, but that paled compared to how he felt now, knowing the truth at last.

And knowing that Anna, the one person he'd trusted so much, the one woman he'd managed to let get under his skin, had known his shame, his secret, the whole time he'd been back here. No wonder she'd tried so hard to convince him Trisha was noble and honorable.

And maybe she was, after all. At least Trisha had tried to get to know him in her own special way. And she'd finally found the courage to tell him the truth. But when he thought back over that first meeting when she'd seemed so jittery, when Anna had made excuses for her, he could see it all there in her face. He remembered snippets of conversation. *You remind me of someone.* Trisha had been trying to tell him. Each time she'd questioned him or even teased him, she'd been trying to get to know her brother. And she'd warned him off Anna, only to turn around and push them together. To appease her own guilt. He had a sister. And Anna had known the whole time.

David stood there, his hands in the pockets of his dress pants, looking up at that shining light. He'd felt the warmth of Anna's strength and her humanity from the first moment he'd met her. He'd felt the light of her goodness and had prayed that some of that light would rub off on him, would make him shine, too.

But David could see now that he had depended on Anna's love and her goodness to pull him through, when deep down inside he needed to pull himself up by his own bootstraps and get on with his life. Now he had come between her and her best friend. He loved Anna but he'd never have a chance to tell her. How could he stay here now?

Anna couldn't sleep. Her blue dress lay discarded across the floral armchair by the big window. She rose to hang it up, only to have something to do. But she stopped to stare out into the night, memories of dancing with David bringing tears to her eyes.

Then she looked down on the street and saw him standing there.

"David," she whispered. She tossed on her clothes and rushed down to see him. Reaching the front door, she swung it open to find him walking away. "David, please wait!"

He kept walking then turned at the end of the driveway.

Anna rushed across the yard to him. "David, I'm so sorry."

"Yeah, me, too," he said, his dark eyes full of a torment that shattered her heart. "Me, too."

"I wanted to tell you, but I promised Trisha—"

"I get it," he said, holding up a hand. "I get all of it now. This is the reason you've been so unsure about me. You were afraid of this, right?"

"I'm not… I was never…unsure about *you*. I was just upset about having to keep this from you. But do you understand how much I've prayed about this, how much I longed to help you?"

He jabbed a finger in the air. "I only understand that Trisha and you knew this and neither of you had the decency to tell me. You let me go on and on about this, Anna. You knew how much I wanted to find him, just to find out who he was. That's all I asked, and yet, you never once let on—" He stopped, biting back the rest of his words, his hands falling to his side.

Anna didn't have the words to explain why she'd stayed silent. How *could* she explain? "I started to tell you so many times, but it wasn't my place to tell you. Trisha needed to be the one. I begged her, advised her, to just sit down with you."

"Right, let's sit poor David down and tell him this sordid little story. Did you both get a big kick out of that?"

Anna's gasp of shock turned to rage. "How could you even think such a thing? You know I'm not that kind of person. I took no pleasure in this. It was tearing me apart. We had to wait until after the party—"

He hit his hands together. "Of course, because nothing can get in the way of rich, powerful people making good on their guilt and their need to show off their riches and their generosity, right? You had to keep things cool until the big event was over. Yeah, that sure makes sense."

"That's unfair," Anna said, tears streaming down her face.

"Yeah, well, my whole life has been unfair, but I had to deal with it, didn't I? My mother and I had to deal with a lot of things after he went away and then got promoted and came back here. Anna, I shook his hand when I was in high school. I shook his hand and looked him in the eye—and he never said a word. Not one word. And neither did you."

He turned to leave then pivoted to stare at her. "You know, I wanted a chance with you. I prayed for that. But I never really had a chance, did I? Now I understand why you were so hesitant and afraid. You knew this about me and you didn't tell me. And that's what hurts me the most. All this time, you let me believe I had a chance."

"David?"

He turned and walked away, his silhouette a disappearing shadow in the dark night.

"David," she whispered, "you had every chance." *And so did you,* she told herself as she stumbled back to the big porch. So did you, Anna. *You should have told him yourself.*

Anna sank down on the swing, tears brimming in her eyes. She tried to form a prayer, but the words became all jumbled in her mind.

The door opened and Olga came out, her hair in

a long braid. "Anna-bug, what are you doing out here at this hour?" Anna couldn't speak, but Olga saw her tears. "What's the matter, darling?"

Anna gulped a response. "I've…I've messed things up. I don't know what to do."

Olga came to sit down beside her, taking Anna in her arms. "Is it David?"

Anna nodded. "He knows, Mother. He knows everything. Trisha told him tonight. And now he blames me. He thinks I can't love him because of who he is, but that's the reason I *do* love him."

"Oh, my poor baby," Olga said, her hand moving through Anna's tousled hair. "My poor, sweet baby. He'll be back. I know he'll be back."

Anna wasn't so sure about that, but because she wanted to cling to that one last hope, she nodded against the warmth of her mother's soft chenille robe. And prayed that Olga was right.

David got up bright and early the next morning. He knew what he had to do. He had to go and see his mother and find out why she'd done this, why she'd never told him who his father really was. And after that, he didn't have a clue where he'd wind up. He'd have to report back to work soon, but that was the only thing he knew for sure.

The phone rang and after checking the caller ID, David answered, trying to keep his tone level. "Hello, Brandon. How's it going?"

"You promised me you'd go see my mother,"

Brandon said, rushed and out of breath. "Don't you remember?"

David silently chastised himself. "I remember. I just got busy. I'll go by today, I promise."

"They're bringing his body home next week," Brandon said. "I kept hoping—"

David's own hurts seemed ridiculous considering what this young man was facing. "Just take care of your mother, Brandon. That's all you can do. Be the best you can be for your mother's sake, you hear me?"

Brandon mumbled an answer. "I gotta go. I'm mowing yards to make some extra money."

David hung up then reached for his Bible. "How am I supposed to comfort this woman, Lord, when I can't even find any comfort myself?"

He searched the pages of his worn Bible, hoping to find the right words there. A passage in Psalms stood out. *Shall not God search this out? For he knoweth the secrets of the heart.*

God had been with David since the beginning, throughout his darkest hours as he lay awake inside a war-torn land. And God had known David's secret, yet He'd brought him home for some reason. David knew he couldn't control life or death or all the pain the two brought, and yet he felt as if he'd been laboring all of his life to do just that. "This life is just a minute," he said, his hand touching on the pages in front of him. "Just a short time." He closed his eyes. "Will I see my father in Heaven, Lord?"

He would have to rely on God as his father.

Maybe he'd been relying on his Heavenly Father all along. How else could he have made it this far?

"Maybe that's how I got through it all," he said as he got up, determined to keep his promise to Brandon. "And maybe that's how I can help Mrs. Matthews and her son, too."

At least it would take his mind off his own troubles.

And the sight of Anna standing there in the dark calling his name as tears streamed down her face.

Chapter Sixteen

"You said if I ever needed to talk—"

Chaplain Steve looked up from his paperwork, surprise evident in his eyes. "David, come on in. Sorry my secretary's at lunch."

"I should have called."

"No, no. That's not necessary. My door is always open. Now let's cut with the small talk and get down to business. You look whipped, my friend."

David sat down then cradled his hands together. "Brandon Matthews wants me to try and console his mother. I'm not sure I'm the right person to do that."

Steve nodded then leaned back in his chair. "Oh, I'd say you're the best man for the job. I hear you and Brandon have bonded over the last few weeks. And I saw you at their house. You've already been a source of comfort for them."

"Yep, Anna and I went together." David blocked out any thoughts of Anna right now. "Brandon and

I were making progress when this happened. But the boy's come a long way in the attitude-adjustment department."

"So you have helped him."

"I guess I have. Mostly because I was so much like him at that age, full of a rage I couldn't even describe. Teenaged angst and all of that. He's just trying to understand why his dad had to be away so long and now, why he had to die."

"We all question that at times," Steve said. "But it's especially hard for a teenager. He'll probably go join up as soon as he's old enough."

David nodded, glanced around at the still-life pictures on the wall. "He's already told me he's going to do just that. I don't know how to explain it to him—the job, the dedication needed, the stress. And I don't think I can talk to his mother right now. It's just hard."

Steve sat silent for a minute then asked, "Is there more to this?"

"A whole lot more," David confessed. "I found out about *my* father. Now I know who he was at least." He held up a hand. "That's all I want to say right now, but it's kind of thrown me for a loop."

"Does your father live nearby? Maybe you need to talk to him, reconcile things."

"He's—he passed away a couple months ago."

"Oh, I'm sorry. That's a shame. I think you could have benefited from seeing him, maybe getting to know him."

"I doubt that," David said, trying to imagine that scene in his head. "What would be the point? The man deserted my mother and me. Left us high and dry."

Steve's expression never wavered, but his eyes held compassion and understanding. "There are always two sides to every story, David. Remember that. Maybe you need to find out more about his side."

"Yeah, maybe, but it's too late to ask him." David shrugged it off for now, his system going on shutdown the way it had done so many times on the front. "What can I say to Brandon's mother? I don't feel very hopeful right now. I've seen too much death, too much of this kind of thing, you know? I'm tired of the shame and the secrets. I'm just so tired."

Steve glanced down to his desk pad. "If you had a second chance with your father, what would you say to him?"

That question jarred David to the core. "I don't know exactly. I guess I'd ask him why he did this to me."

"Remember how Christ had that moment of doubt on the cross when He cried out to God?"

David nodded. "Yes, but—"

"But He followed through anyway. He did His duty by taking the weight of the world onto His shoulders. He suffered for our sins."

"I understand that, but I don't see the connection."

"The connection is that while your father didn't follow through the way he was supposed to with his responsibility toward you, you did follow through, David. You've been a good and faithful servant, doing a job that most men wouldn't attempt. And since you've been home, you've tried to help everyone around you in some small way. So while you might think you were betrayed by your own father, Christ has been right there with you every step of the way because you show His example on a daily basis. And that's the hope you can give to Brandon and his mother. They can turn to the Lord in their hour of need, and so can you, my friend. Their pain can't be fixed, but it can be listened to and heard. And so can your own. You just need someone to acknowledge that. You need someone to see into your soul and heal your wounds. Christ can give you that reassurance."

"But that's obvious," David replied, thinking of Psalms. "I've tried to turn to Him so many times. Only this time, I'm not so sure I can accept the answers I've been given. But then, having my prayers answered doesn't exactly mean I like what I hear, right?"

"There are never easy answers," Steve admitted with a smile. "But maybe you need to consider the not-so-obvious. Maybe you need to consider the other side of things. There is always a reason for everything in life. And I'm sure your parents had their reasons for doing what they did, whether you want to hear those reasons or not."

David toyed with a fray on his pants leg. "They had an affair and then he left my mother alone and pregnant. I think that pretty much says it all."

"Are you sure? Or have you been so busy blaming them that you haven't even bothered finding out the truth?"

"It was Commander Morrison, okay?" David blurted out. "He's my father and Trisha is my half sister. She told me everything the night of the ball. And Anna knew it all along."

Steve pulled a hand down his face. "That certainly makes it hard to accept."

David pounded his fist against the desk. "Yes, it sure does. If I stay here, I'll have to see her every day and I'll have to remember that her fine and upstanding father never acknowledged me. How can I live with that? And to top it off, I've lost Anna because of this." He shook his head, staring down at his hands. "I can't deal with it anymore."

Steve let him stew for a while, then said, "All this time, you've been focused on finding out your father's identity. Maybe you should have concentrated on finding out his motives, and your mother's, too. Everyone deserves a second chance, David. Maybe it's time you give yourself a second chance by finding out the other truth—the one behind all the lies and silence. I think you need to give Trisha a second chance, too. If anyone needs an older brother right now, it's Trisha. Try to look at the good in this, instead of the bad."

David's retort wasn't kind. "Why should she need me? She's got it all. She had his love, his devotion and now she has status and honor. Me, I have some paltry trust fund that my mother refused even to tell me about until I was older. I don't care about the money, but I do care about the lies."

"Have you ever considered that God brought you back here, though, for just that very reason? Trisha puts up a good front, and yes, on the surface her life looks pretty rosy, but she's alone and afraid and she's made some bad moves lately. Think about how you could help each other. You can be bitter or you can see this as an opportunity to heal. As I said, a second chance."

David looked over at his friend, a light dawning inside his tired, numb brain. "Funny, I just told Anna that very same thing the other night. She was worried about her mother and I told her everyone deserves a second chance."

"Funny, isn't it," Steve said with a grin, "how life works that way?"

"Anna, what should I do about lunch for the day care? The volunteer scheduled to help cook today called in sick. Anna?"

Anna looked around to find her secretary standing at her door. "Oh, I'm sorry, Laura. What did you say?"

"The day care—one of the cooks is sick."

Anna shuffled some papers. "Let's call Mrs. Hughes. She'll pull together something wonderful. I'll call her right away."

Laura came in and sat down across from Anna. "Is something wrong? You've been staring out the window for about five minutes."

Anna shifted back in her chair, fatigue pulling at

her shoulders. "No, nothing's wrong. I've just got some things on my mind. I can't seem to get any information about Whitney and John and I keep getting calls from reporters wanting to do another background story on them. I've just about exhausted all of my resources. Every time we think we've found evidence that they've been taken, it runs dry."

Laura touched a hand to her blond hair, twirling it as she frowned. "They've been missing for weeks now. Do you think something bad has happened? I mean, *were* they taken hostage?"

"That's a possibility," Anna replied, telling herself to stay focused, telling herself she had people waiting for her help, people to call about funding, children to comfort. And a heart that was broken, a heart that would always be broken. She'd tried so hard to fix things for everyone else, but what about herself? What could she possibly do to fix things for herself now that David was out of her life? And she'd pushed him away. Trisha was right; Anna had used the excuse of Trisha's secret to keep David at arm's length. Simply because she'd hidden her heart away, afraid to love too much.

"Their picture is up on the Wall of Hope," Laura said, referring to the long wall at Prairie Springs Christian Church where copies of letters and pictures between soldiers and children here at home were displayed. "Caitlyn is being careful not to tell the twins that they're missing."

Anna thought about little Amanda and Josie and

how they'd been so excited to "adopt" John and Whitney after the deaths of their own parents. Always death, always sadness. She wondered if she could take another step. "She told me she allows them to draw pictures anyway. She plans on keeping them in case…" Anna felt hot tears pricking at her eyes as she took a deep breath. "Maybe if I do talk to some of the reporters and they put out a story, maybe someone over there will see it and give us hope. Or a least let us know they're alive and safe."

Laura got up. "Why don't you let me call Mrs. Hughes. Want me to shut your door?"

Anna shook her head. "No. I'll be fine. Just having a bad morning."

Was it a sin, Lord, to hold back information from David? Did I do the right thing?

Telling herself the important issue was that David and Trisha could now start fresh, Anna tried to put her own heartache on hold. But in her secret heart, she prayed David would forgive her for her part in all of this.

Then Brandon came through the front door, his eyes wide as he stammered and shifted on his tennis shoes. "He left, Anna. David left without even coming by to see my mother and me yet. Where did he go?"

David stood in front of the Matthews home, thinking the modest little house on post represented the kind of life he'd often dreamed of growing up. He'd purposely come here without telling Brandon because he wanted to see Mrs. Matthews alone. But he still didn't have the words to express this bone-deep grief that seemed to want to weigh him down. Maybe he was having some sort of post-traumatic episode.

The front door opened with a squeak, then Mrs. Matthews walked out onto the tiny porch. "David, I thought that was you." Her smile was soft, her eyes red-rimmed and bloodshot. "Do you think if you stand out here long enough, you'll find the right words for me, son?"

David saw the compassion in the widow's eyes and almost crumpled to the ground right there. Holding his head up high, he said, "Can we talk?"

She motioned to an old glider on the porch. "Have a seat."

David followed her to the swing, then settled in beside her as she automatically started rocking, each squeak of the rusty metal glider sounding off with a perfect cadence.

"Brandon wanted me to come by," he said, hoping being honest would help him get through this. "He doesn't know I'm here."

"He's trying so hard to fill his father's shoes," she said, her hand holding to the glider arm. "I've tried to tell him I'll be okay, but he's taking this so hard."

"It is hard," David said, listening to a child's laughter somewhere down the tree-shaded street. "When someone dies, it's like your own heart gets a tear in it."

"And you don't know how to fix the tear."

"No, you don't." He took a long, shuddering

breath. "I never knew my father and the burden of that has finally caught up with me, I think."

Mrs. Matthews touched her hand to his in a motherly pat. "Want to talk about it?"

David swallowed back all the denial in his soul. "Yes, ma'am, I think I do."

And so he poured out his heart to this gentle widow who held his hand and patted it throughout his sad tale. And when he was finished, it was she who comforted him.

Two hours later, David heard a knock on his door.

Brandon stood there, staring up at him with an expression that bordered on both censure and relief.

"She told me you came by. I thought you'd left, man."

"I am leaving," David said as he motioned the boy in. "I'm going to see my own mother."

"Oh, okay." Brandon shifted on his big feet, his gaze moving over David's sparse apartment. "You don't hang around very long, do you?"

"I guess I don't." He rolled his shoulders. "I had hoped to stay here a while though."

"Are you gonna do that? Or are you getting out while you can? Anna said you'd had some personal troubles. She looked real sad."

David sat down on the couch. "Anna told you the truth. I have to work through some things, but I'm not running away, Brandon. I just need to go visit my mother."

"Well, thanks for coming by. Mom said you had a good talk. She seemed better."

"Your mother is a strong woman. She is so proud of you and of your dad. He was a hero, Brandon. The best this country has to offer."

Brandon leaned back against the wall. "Do you think I could ever be like that?"

David looked up at the boy in front of him, wondering how many sons had asked themselves that same question. How many times had he wondered that about himself? "I think you're well on your way, but like I told you, do it for all the right reasons." Then he shrugged. "Or maybe doing it for all the wrong reasons will eventually make things right. Maybe that's what makes a hero."

His heart did a funny little lurch as he thought about Anna. She'd held Trisha's secret for all the right reasons. She hadn't betrayed him; she'd tried not to betray her friend. But in the end, David knew, just as Anna had, that Trisha would have had to be the one to tell him the truth.

So why was he punishing Anna? Maybe because, just like his mother, she'd withheld something precious and dear from him. But it hadn't been the truth about his father. It had been her heart and her love. He could see that so clearly now. And he realized Anna's love was worth fighting for.

Brandon rubbed his hand over his stomach. "Got time for a pizza?"

David grinned as an unfamiliar peace seemed to

settle over his soul. "I think I do. I'm not leaving until early tomorrow morning."

He'd go and clear the air with his mother once and for all. And when he got back home, he'd clear things with Anna, too.

Chapter Seventeen

David was once again standing in front of a modest house, wondering what words he'd use when he entered the door. Only this one was hundreds of miles away from Prairie Springs, in northwest Louisiana. Telling himself he could do this, he closed his eyes and heard the hum of a chopper's great whirling blades inside his head. He felt the hot desert wind on his flushed skin and he heard another kind of roar inside his ears, the roar of battle and adrenaline and fear and hope all rolled up into one long rumble of intensity. And he prayed for peace, inside the war zone and inside his own bruised and battered heart.

"David?"

David opened his eyes to find his mother standing at the door, her hands over her mouth. Sandra Ryland looked old. His mother had always dyed her red hair to a strawberry blond, but now it just looked brassy and thin. She'd gained a few pounds, making her soft around the edges. David had always remembered her as a hard enlistee, sometimes silent and noncommunicative and other times laughing and comical. But now he could see the wear and tear of her long-held secrets right there in his mother's blue eyes. And he could see the tears falling down her cheeks.

"Davie, is that really you? You finally came to see me?"

David nodded, tears piercing his eyes. "I'm here, Mom. I'm finally here."

It had been the longest journey of his life.

"He's been gone almost a week now."

Anna whispered to Trisha as they stood at the Wall of Hope, reading over the copies of letters from soldiers to the children around the post and in Prairie Springs who had been corresponding with them. Olga copied the letters and pictures the children created then sent the originals to the soldiers. Whenever a soldier wrote back, she'd make a copy of that, too, to put on the wall, making sure the children got the original.

Being here, reading the words of heartfelt thanks and prayers, always brought on her own tug-of-war inside Anna's soul. She had long ago accepted that war was a necessary part of life, but sometimes she had a hard time finding reasons to believe. And today, that feeling of loss and despair was raging with all the fieriness of a great battle inside her heart and inside her head. She missed David so much it hurt to think about him. Maybe that was why she felt so out of sorts this morning. Not one to burst into tears often, Anna felt as if she might do just that if she had to read one more sad letter.

"He survived all of this, Trisha, only to come home to his own kind of battle. I just wish I knew whether he's safe or not."

"You miss him," Trisha said in the same low tone Anna had used, echoing Anna's own thoughts. "Believe it or not, I miss him, too. And it's all my fault that he left us."

"It's no one's fault," Anna countered. "He had to know and you did the right thing, telling him."

"Ah, but I told him in a moment of frustration on a night when I should have left you two alone to enjoy each other."

Anna closed her eyes, remembering the sweetness of being in David's arms. "It was a wonderful night, or at least it started out that way. But it's over now. I have to get back to what matters here and that means I need to keep working. So I'm going to search for more ways to get help with finding Whitney and John. Evan was just in here and he's not taking it so well." The two young soldiers were still missing somewhere in the Middle East, lost somewhere inside the war zone. She touched a hand to Whitney's image, thinking about how worried Whitney's older brother was. "We're all scarred in some way by war, aren't we?"

Trisha nodded then put an arm on Anna's shoulder.

"How can anyone take this kind of news? Evan loves his sister and Whitney was—is—one of the sweetest people I know. We're all praying for them."

Anna leaned close to read one of the letters Olga had helped Amanda and Josie write to John and Whitney just a couple of weeks ago:

> We hope you are safe. Do you get good food?
> Do you have pizza and ice cream? When you get
> home, we can have a picnic. Would you like that?

Such simple questions, yet they told a lifetime of words, a lifetime of children's giggles and hopes. How could any of them cope if the newlyweds were lost forever?

Olga came around the corner and spotted them there. "Hello, my lovelies. Any word, Anna?"

"No." Anna turned to smile at her mother. "How are you?"

Olga glanced behind her. "I had a pleasant lunch with Franklin today. I think he's warming up to me."

"It's Franklin now, is it?" Trisha asked, whispering again. "I'd say things are progressing nicely."

Olga shrugged. "I've been alone over twenty years. I can be patient."

But the faraway look in her eyes told Anna her mother was worried this morning, too. Maybe the good reverend had picked up on that and had decided to offer Olga his own form of kindness.

Anna hoped her mother would find some sort of

happiness, but she had to wonder if the stoic minister was the right person to give Olga the security she needed. Then again, maybe Reverend Fields could have a calming effect on her vivacious mother.

Olga's smile brought her out of her musings. "What about you, Anna-bug? Have you heard from David?"

Anna shook her head. "Brandon told me he's gone to see his mother." She glanced over at Trisha. "I can only imagine that meeting can't be easy."

Trisha turned to lean back on a table. "I tried calling him, but no answer. Do you think he'll ever forgive me, Miss Olga?"

Olga brushed a hand over Trisha's hair. "What's to forgive, darling? You can't help who your parents were and you can't change what happened between David's mother and your father. But you can do your best to show David the love he never received as a child. You can be the sister he needs you to be." She gave Anna a long glance. "We can all work to show David that he was never abandoned. He was meant to come right back here to us. But I think he had to get to this place all on his own."

Anna wondered how she was supposed to show David that kind of love and support when he wouldn't even give her a chance.

Then she heard the door opening at the end of the long hall and saw him walking toward her.

David braced himself. He was a coward when it came to showing his emotions, but he had to do this.

He had to get Anna back. And he also needed to work on getting to know his new sister. He was tired of shutting himself off from everyone who loved him.

"Hi," he said, his eyes on Anna.

"Hi." She glanced over at Trisha.

David turned to his sister. "I need to talk to you later, but right now, I want to talk to Anna. Alone."

Olga patted her hair, her smile smug. "Trisha, I could use some help mixing the punch for the support-group meeting."

Trisha nodded, her wide dark eyes holding David's gaze. She started toward Olga then pivoted back to David. "I'm glad you're home."

David took Anna to his truck and without speaking, started driving for the spot at the lake. He could feel her eyes on him, could sense that she needed to say things. But he wasn't ready to speak. Right now, he just wanted to know she was near.

When they reached the lake, he came around the truck to open her door and their eyes met. "David—"

He held up a hand. "Do you want to know why I come here? Why I came here to this spot when I was young?"

She nodded as she got out and shut the door.

He didn't touch her, just guided her to their spot. "When I first discovered this place, I'd just had a horrible fight with my mom. I stole her car and just took off and this is where I wound up." He pointed toward the hills to the west. "I watched the sun setting over the sky and I wondered if that same sun was shining on my father's face somewhere in the world. I just wanted to know that I had something, anything to share with the man. I needed that connection."

He heard her inhale a soft breath, but he didn't dare look at her. "I didn't feel whole. I never felt whole. Even till the very day I came back here. I came back for answers, but instead I…I found you." Then he turned to face her. "I found you, Anna. And even after everything I've been through, after thinking I needed that missing half of my life, it wasn't my father I was searching for. It was you all the time. You're the one I came back to find, without knowing I'd even find you. *You* made me feel whole again on that first day when you took my hand in yours. You *make* me feel as if nothing else matters."

She tried to speak, but he touched a finger to her lips. "You were there, smiling at me, thanking me for what I'd done. So simple, but it made a difference to me. It made it all worth the trip. I trusted your smile, your kindness. I saw the goodness shining in your eyes. And then I watched you with the children in the nursery, with the upset mothers sitting in the lobby. I saw you had this incredible gift of making other people feel better about things. You made me feel that way."

She swallowed back the tears he saw in her eyes, took his hand in hers. "David…"

"Don't tell me you're sorry," he said, closing his eyes. "You don't have to be sorry. This wasn't your fault."

"But, you see, it was. I blamed Trisha's secret for keeping us apart when it was really my own doubts and fears. I'm out of excuses, David."

"I know," he said, his smile indulgent. "And so am I. But it's going to be all right now."

She held a fist against her face, pressing it into the spot between her nose and her mouth. "You saw your mother?"

"Yeah. We got it all cleared up." He let her hold on to his hand while he stared out at the water. "She told me that my dad loved me. She sent him updates all the time, right up until the very end. He always had a private post office box just for her and according to her, he followed my every move. And she gave me letters he'd written to me."

"Why didn't he ever—"

"He loved us as much as he loved his wife, but he also felt obligated to her. Apparently, Trisha's mother was very fragile and…ill. After I was born, he and my mother decided to keep their secret because of that. My mother knew how much he loved her, but she also knew she couldn't break up his marriage. When his wife got pregnant, he was so happy but he was afraid if she found out about us, she'd lose the baby. He had a reputation to maintain. So…in all those years my mother didn't force things. She allowed him to stay with his wife. She told him that she'd raise me and make him proud. And that's what she tried to do. He sent money to the trust fund and he went on with his life. They both agreed that no one would ever know.

Then his wife died and he felt guilty, so he wrote the letter to Trisha. And now we all know."

Anna finally spoke, but her voice was husky and hoarse. "That was a tremendous burden to put on Trisha and you. I wish there could have been a better way."

David turned to her then, tugging her into his arms. "There was a better way. You, Anna. You were the buffer, the link between Trisha and me. And everyone I've told about this only had one thing to say. Chaplain Steve, my mother, even Brandon's mom—they all told me that everyone deserves a second chance."

He hated the tears falling down her face. He reached up a finger to catch one, its warmth washing over him like a cleansing river. "Even me," he added, his fingers lingering on her cheeks. "Even me. Will you give me that chance?"

"Yes." Anna reached up and pulled him close. "I love you, David."

"I love you, too."

They shared a kiss, the rustling of the trees mixing with the sound of water moving against the rocks down below. And all the other sounds, all the other roaring white-hot memories that usually cluttered David's mind, seemed to recede into the background until all he could hear was the sweet rhythm of Anna's heart beating so close to his own.

"Are we going to be okay?" she asked.

He nodded. "I think we're going to be just fine, Chief. I'm finally home."

* * *

When David dropped Anna back off at the church, Trisha's sports car was still there. Smiling at Anna, he said, "I'll come by later. How 'bout we have a nice dinner at Carmella's?"

She grinned, her heart healing with each touch, with each kiss. "That sounds great." Then she turned serious. "What about Trisha?"

"I'm going to find her right now." He kissed her on the nose. "My baby sister and I have a lot of catching up to do."

The side door of the church opened and Trisha came out with a hesitant look on her face. Anna watched as David opened his arms to her. Trisha grinned then burst into tears as her brother hugged her close.

Epilogue

Later that afternoon, David and Anna were sitting in Anna's office. She was finishing up some paperwork before dinner. The front door rattled open and in walked Jake Hopkins.

"Jake, how are you?" Anna asked, standing to shake his hand. "David, this is General Willis's attorney, Jake Hopkins. He helped all of us figure out how to get Ali over here."

"Hello. Nice to meet you," David said. "Thanks for all you did for Ali."

Jake held on to his cane, his dark gaze sweeping the room. "I had to learn as I went—didn't have a clue as to how to handle all that immigration red tape. But don't tell the general that." Then he shook his head. "Ali is something else—worth all my sweat. That boy's as tough as his ornery old grandfather."

Anna smiled over at David. "Isn't it great how

Sarah's stepped in to help? She and Ali have really hit it off."

Jake grunted. "Yeah, well, Marlon needs all the help he can get." He placed some papers on Anna's desk. "Can't stay. Just wanted to drop off the files on that pro bono case I've been helping y'all with."

"Thanks," Anna said. When the door opened yet again she began to wonder if she'd be able get away to have a romantic dinner with David after all.

Madeline Bright bounced down the hallway, waving as she went. "I'll be back in a minute. Just bringing in some school supplies." She did a double take when she saw Jake, but she kept on going.

Jake grabbed his cane, his gaze sliding off Maddie and back to Anna with a panicked look.

"Do you know Maddie?" Anna asked. "She helped escort Ali here. I can introduce you."

She got up, but Jake waved her back in her chair. "No, I'm late for an appointment." He ran a hand over his dark hair then glanced around toward the door. "I'll meet her another time. Like I said, I've got to get going."

Jake looked so uncomfortable Anna couldn't help but shoot a questioning look at David. When they heard Maddie laughing in another room, Jake hurried toward the door, his cane hitting the hardwood floor with a tap, tap, tap that echoed long after he'd shut the door.

Maddie came back up the hall. "He sure was in a hurry. Is it just me, or did he seem strange?"

"Jake? He has some odd quirks, but he's one of the good guys," Anna assured the young nurse. "He's the lawyer who took care of all the legalities of getting Ali here."

"Hmm." Maddie's smile dimmed for a second, then she said, "Oh, I forgot. I wanted to give you this check. All the nurses on my floor got together to buy the school supplies, but we also collected this financial donation. We wanted to do something for Children of the Day."

Anna looked at the hefty amount. "Thanks, Maddie. This will go a long way. We've almost reached our budget goal for next year and this will help."

Maddie smiled then looked at David. "Glad to be home, Chief?"

David lifted a brow toward Anna. "I sure am. How about you?"

Maddie tossed him a look over her shoulder. "I'm doing okay," she said. "But I think I'm about to shake things up around here. I might have to get to know that quirky lawyer a little bit better. He's cute in a ruffled kind of way."

Anna and David laughed at her jaunty exit.

"Think there could be some kind of flirtation developing?" David asked. "Maddie was beaming like a spotlight just talking about Jake."

"Maddie and Jake?" Anna giggled at the thought. "That might be interesting. Maddie is a ball of fire, but Jake, well, he's kind of rough around the edges."

David pulled her up out of her chair then tugged her close. "So was I, remember?"

"But not anymore," she said as he lowered his head.

"Not anymore," he replied, just before kissing her. "I never thought I'd say this, but it is so good to be back in the Lone Star state."

Anna certainly agreed with that sentiment. She gave him a peck on the cheek. "Now, how about that dinner? I'm starving."

David laughed as he tugged her toward the door. "You're the boss, Chief."

"And don't you forget it," Ann said, laughing as she grabbed her tote bag.

Through the tall windows of her office, the late-afternoon sunshine fell like a soft spotlight across the worn Bible lying on her desk. David touched a hand to the Bible then kissed her on the cheek.

The front door opened as they were headed toward it. Trisha rushed in, looking from David to Anna. "Oh, were you about to leave?"

"We're going out for dinner," Anna said. Then she sent a questioning look toward David.

"You want to come?" he said, regret tingeing the question. But he had an indulgent smile on his face.

Trisha shook her head. "I am not going to be a third wheel around you two, but I do need a favor."

"What's that?" David asked, already falling into his big-brother mode.

"I'm taking flowers out to my father's grave," Trisha said as she twisted the strap of her purse. "Would you like to go with me?"

David looked from Trisha to Anna. "Sure. I'd like to go."

Anna patted him on the arm. "I'll meet you at the restaurant then."

"No," David said, taking her by the hand as he put his other hand on Trisha's arm. "Let's all three go together. We'll go to the cemetery, and then let's go by and visit Ali before dinner."

An hour later, they stood in the quiet cemetery up on a hill just outside of town staring down at Commander Morrison's grave. The spray of colorful yellow and burgundy mums and baby's breath Trisha had brought gave a sense of life to the lonely hillside grave.

"He wanted to be buried here," Trisha said, her arm linked in David's. "That was important to him, to be buried with my mother." She glanced up at David, her gaze searching his face. "Does that bother you?"

"No," David said, his heart at peace now.

Anna leaned against him on the other side, her strength bringing David the love and contentment he'd been searching for all his life. "Isn't it amazing, that we're all here together? I'm so glad you two found each other."

David kissed her on the head then tugged Trisha close. "Yes, pretty amazing. If it hadn't been for Ali, I might not have come back here. I guess I owe that little boy a lot. He changed my life."

"Let's go see him," Trisha said, swiping at tears.

David let go then nodded toward his truck. "Go on. I'll be up in a minute."

Anna nodded, waiting for Trisha to follow her.

He watched until they had crested the hill then turned to look down at his father's grave again. "I know you had your reasons, sir, and I can respect that now. I just wish I could have known you. But I promise you this—I will watch over Trisha and try to be a good brother to her. And when Anna and I have a child, I'll try to be a good father. I guess it really is never too late for second chances."

Then he stepped back, saluted and turned with a soldier's straight back to go find the sister he'd just discovered. And the woman he loved.

* * * * *

*In September 2008, don't miss
the third* HOMECOMING HEROES *book,
AT HIS COMMAND by Brenda Coulter.*

Dear Reader:

I feel so blessed to have been a part of this series, *Homecoming Heroes*. The plot and the actual writing were both very challenging, but being able to learn more about what our soldiers go through each day has made me a lot more patriotic. I researched everything from the front lines to getting the wounded off the battlefield and to a hospital and, finally, home to America. It is not an easy process, but it is something that happens every day in a war. Please know that any mistakes in my story were my own.

David and Anna were such diverse characters. They both had past hurts because of their fathers. In Anna's case, her father had died in a war so she took it upon herself to try and help those who suffered from war. David had never known his military father so that became the driving force behind his desire to fight. But in the end, he realized he'd been fighting against God's love and the stigma of not having a dad. Anna's gentle love showed him that God was on his side.

I hope you enjoy this series, and know that if you have a loved one serving our country, you should be very proud. They are all in my prayers.

Until next time, may the angels watch over you. Always.

Lenora Worth

QUESTIONS FOR DISCUSSION

1. Why did David return to Fort Bonnell? Do you believe people should return to the past in order to change the future? What incidents from your past have shaped who you are today? Discuss.

2. What made Anna start Children of the Day? How do you think pouring oneself into a project hides one's pain? What other coping mechanisms might Anna have used? What would you have done in her situation?

3. Olga was a gregarious character. Do you know someone who is a true Christian but also a very colorful person? How has this person shown you God's love?

4. Do you think Ali's grandfather did the right thing by helping to bring him to America? How did the little boy help bring the town of Prairie Springs together?

5. General Willis was once a hardhearted soldier. How did Ali help to soften him? Do you think God brings children into our lives so that we can soften toward His love? What positive influences have you seen children play in other people's lives?

6. What was holding Anna back from loving David? What might be holding you back from receiving God's love?

7. David came back with a mission to find out the truth. Do you think it's wise to delve into the past? Or is it better to leave things in the past? How can turning to God help with this decision?

8. Trisha had a lot of love in her heart but she wasn't sure how to focus that love on something good. How did David's return help her to do that? What lesson did Trisha have to learn in order to be able to tell David the truth?

9. Do you think David and Trisha will become close? How did their faith help them to find each other and forgive their parents' indiscretions?

10. Do you think Olga's intentions in flirting with the minister were right? Do you think a man of God can find true happiness with a woman late in life? How do you think Olga could (or should) have courted the minister differently?

11. What did Anna realize after David found out the truth? Why was she using Trisha's secret as an excuse not to love David?

12. Do you believe Anna was right in keeping Trisha's secret? Have you ever had to keep such a secret even though you felt confused and unsure about doing so? How can prayer help in this situation?

13. It is very hard for a returning soldier to get back into ordinary daily routines. Why is it so important for someone returning from war to turn to God?

14. Do you believe God can truly heal all wounds, both physical and the deep wounds of the soul? David had to learn this lesson when Brandon's father was killed. How did he help Brandon? And how did Brandon's mother help David?

Only one person knows why Kat Thatcher left her Oklahoma hometown ten years ago. That person is Seth Washington. And now that she's back, he's only too available to talk about the past. Seth insists the Lord is on their side and always was. But will that be enough for love?

Look for

A Time To Heal

by

Linda Goodnight

Available September wherever books are sold, including most bookstores, supermarkets, drugstores and discount stores.

www.SteepleHill.com

Steeple Hill®

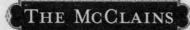

REQUEST YOUR FREE BOOKS!

2 FREE INSPIRATIONAL NOVELS
PLUS 2
FREE
MYSTERY GIFTS

Love Inspired®

YES! Please send me 2 FREE Love Inspired® novels and my 2 FREE mystery gifts (gifts are worth about $10). After receiving them, if I don't wish to receive any more books, I can return the shipping statement marked "cancel". If I don't cancel, I will receive 4 brand-new novels every month and be billed just $4.24 per book in the U.S. or $4.74 per book in Canada, plus 25¢ shipping and handling per book and applicable taxes, if any*. That's a savings of over 20% off the cover price! I understand that accepting the 2 free books and gifts places me under no obligation to buy anything. I can always return a shipment and cancel at any time. Even if I never buy another book, the two free books and gifts are mine to keep forever.

113 IDN ERXA   313 IDN ERWX

Name _____ (PLEASE PRINT) _____

Address _____ Apt. # _____

City _____ State/Prov. _____ Zip/Postal Code _____

Signature (if under 18, a parent or guardian must sign)

Order online at www.LoveInspiredBooks.com

Or mail to Steeple Hill Reader Service:

IN U.S.A.: P.O. Box 1867, Buffalo, NY 14240-1867
IN CANADA: P.O. Box 609, Fort Erie, Ontario L2A 5X3

Not valid to current subscribers of Love Inspired books.

Want to try two free books from another series?
Call 1-800-873-8635 or visit www.morefreebooks.com

* Terms and prices subject to change without notice. N.Y. residents add applicable sales tax. Canadian residents will be charged applicable provincial taxes and GST. Offer not valid in Quebec. This offer is limited to one order per household. All orders subject to approval. Credit or debit balances in a customer's account(s) may be offset by any other outstanding balance owed by or to the customer. Please allow 4 to 6 weeks for delivery. Offer available while quantities last.

Your Privacy: Steeple Hill Books is committed to protecting your privacy. Our Privacy Policy is available online at www.SteepleHill.com or upon request from the Reader Service. From time to time we make our lists of customers available to reputable third parties who may have a product or service of interest to you. If you would prefer we not share your name and address, please check here. ☐

LIREG08R

HOMECOMING
★ HEROES ★

**Saving children and finding love
deep in the heart of Texas!**

Look for these six heart-warming Homecoming Heroes stories!

Mission: Motherhood by Marta Perry
July 2008

Lone Star Secret by Lenora Worth
August 2008

At His Command by Brenda Coulter
September 2008

A Matter of the Heart by Patricia Davids
October 2008

A Texas Thanksgiving by Margaret Daley
November 2008

Homefront Holidays by Jillian Hart
December 2008

Available wherever books are sold.

Steeple
Hill®

www.SteepleHill.com

LIHHLIST

TITLES AVAILABLE NEXT MONTH

Don't miss these four stories in September

A DRY CREEK COURTSHIP by Janet Tronstad
Dry Creek
Charley Nelson wants more than friendship with Edith Hargrove.
He wants romance. But the no-nonsense widow misunderstands,
and starts lining up candidates for him to date! How can he
convince her that she's the only woman for him?

AT HIS COMMAND by Brenda Coulter
Homecoming Heroes
Everyone in Prairie Springs loves cheerful army nurse
Madeline Bright. Yet the only man to catch her eye is ex-pilot
Jake Hopkins. Jake is convinced she's better off without him,
but Maddie is determined to be part of his life. And if he's not
careful, she might conquer his heart.

A TIME TO HEAL by Linda Goodnight
Years ago, Kat Thatcher fled her hometown with a secret only
Seth Washington knew. Now she's back, and comes face-to-face
with Seth on her first day in town! He's as handsome as ever, and
available. Way too available for a woman who isn't sure she's
ready to love again.

DEEP IN THE HEART by Jane Myers Perrine
Katie Wallace left Silver Lake with big dreams...and came home
with big heartache. Silver Lake has gone on without her—so has
Rob Chambers, the boy she left behind. Can Rob forgive her and
give them both a second chance at love?

LICNM0808